THE EXCLUSIVE

Girl Reporter Book #1

JESSICA GLASNER

HOPE
HOUSE

First Printing: 9798666230176

Hope House Press
www.hopehousepress.co
www.glasnerhouse.co

HISTORICAL NOTE

In the Spring of 1940, Europe was in the thick of war. The Nazis were invading countries left and right. Many of Europe's Jewish population were fighting tooth and nail to survive. Most Americans, however, were reluctant to jump into the fray. "Let Europe deal with her own problems!" and "Why put our lives on the line to clean up someone else's mess?" were the general attitudes of the day.

Why was this the general attitude? What did the American public think was happening in Germany?

They thought what the media told them to think—all of which was highly censored. This was especially true when it came to the movies.

There is evidence to suggest that many Hollywood studios collaborated with the Nazis by refusing to make films that showed the Nazis in a negative light or defended the Jews. Whether this collaboration was formal or simply a way studios tried to cope with an increasingly tense situation overseas does not negate their actions (or lack thereof). Between 1939 and 1941, only a handful of American films were made that were anti-Nazi or pro-British. The fact also remains that during these years, many American officials (who understood the innate power of film to move the public to action), prevented films that could be construed as "interventionist" (or pro-America joining the war) from being produced. Because of their preventive measures, the truth of the evil surging in and spreading beyond Germany's borders was largely hidden from the American public.

Considering today's world of "fake news" and "alternative facts," this relatively unknown yet corresponding period in our history is particularly meaningful. In the words of Robert McKee, "No civilization . . . has ever been destroyed because they know too much truth."[1] And in the words of Jesus, "The truth will set you free" (John 8:32, ESV).

I based this story on historical records and real political and military events. However, the characters are fictional unless otherwise noted.

CHAPTER 1

Help Wanted

My room looked down on the garden. Once, it grew beautiful Scottish primrose and bluebells, dwarf cornels and mountain avens.

Now the flowers were gone, ploughed under to grow vegetables (potatoes, cabbages, and rutabagas) to help with the war effort. Our cook, Mrs. Butterfield, in addition to leading the re-landscaping mission, ran the local chapter of the *Women's Institute,* an organization whose motto was "Plant for victory! Keep the Germans out by growing vitamins at our door." As much as I agreed about keeping the Germans out, I much preferred the bluebells to rutabagas.

Beyond the garden was a great, green lawn, lined with pine, birch, and sprawling oak trees. The trees and the lawn were practically sacred, and Mrs. Butterfield was strictly forbidden from touching them.

That particular spring morning, I lay in my bed looking up at the ceiling, listening to the sound of bagpipes blown by three of the oldest boys on the lawn. Every morning, rain or shine, the boys were on that green rectangle, jogging in place and doing calisthenics before breakfast to the rhythm of the pipes. It was quite the wake-up call.

There were forty-three children altogether. Forty were from a boarding school for boys that transferred into our house, along with three wizened old tutors, when the Germans began to pummel London with bombs (and the younger teachers were drafted). The other three were Jewish refugees—twin boys and a girl—from Holland. These we'd rescued on the last voyage of my Uncle Horatio's yacht, the *Grey Goose*, in the summer of 1939.

What a summer that had been! The summer my mother had miraculously recovered from tuberculosis. The summer Edie had *finally* married Horatio. The summer we'd left the States for Europe. The summer I'd fallen in love with Peter, Horatio's nephew and my best friend in the whole world. And the summer we'd all come to the north of Scotland. In the meantime, my aunt had fallen in love with Anna, Willem, and

Raffi and would have adopted them if she could. She couldn't, of course, because their parents were still alive (we hoped), and they'd have to go back to them once the war ended.

It was a very different life from the one I'd had growing up in California. The life where I'd gone to school on weekdays and the movies on Saturday night. A time when my mother and I had always been off shopping and rollerskating, living easy days full of fun, while my father worked at his small but successful medical practice in town. That life seemed a million miles away and a thousand years ago.

My father now spent his days treating the village people (there weren't many) and the boys from the school in a small clinic he'd set up in Horatio's old carriage house. Edie, days away from having a baby, was on strict bedrest, leaving only my mother, Ferguson (Horatio's butler and the air-warden for all of Kingsbarns since the war began), and myself to take care of the house and three-year-old Anna. It was just us because the maids had been drafted too, like the teachers from the school in London. Almost all able-bodied women were in some sort of work for the war in one way or another. Whether they took over the farms or went to the factories to build planes or parachutes, domestic servants were few and far between.[1]

On top of everything else, there wasn't a high school in Kingsbarns, and I still had two classes left before I graduated, so I plodded along via correspondence. (All the boys who came were twelve and younger, so it was pointless to join in their classes, though one of the old tutors did help me with my trigonometry.)

It seemed to me that all I did in those days was study and clean up. And I seemed to be making little progress in either department. I was *not* a "math person" and trying to keep this particular house clean was a losing battle. Even though the boys did their own laundry, helped with the dishes, and kept their dormitory on the fourth floor clean, under the supervision of their tutors, an estate like Horatio's was meant to be cleaned by more than just my mother, a butler, and a part-time student/girl-reporter for *The Scotsman* who covered the exceptionally boring county of Kingsbarns. (Nothing ever happened here except for the occasional festival where I *might* get to shoot a picture of a prize-winning unnaturally fat sheep, as I had the previous weekend. There wasn't even a movie theater! The best we had in the entertainment department was the ancient projector Horatio set up on occasion. But even then, we only had a few old silent films from twenty years ago that Edie'd found in the attic.

It had been months since I've been with anyone near my age. My cousins Katrine, Grace, and Lorelei were knee-deep in some field in Palestine "reclaiming the land" as part of the "Youth Aliyah Movement," and Peter, who I planned to marry the minute I turned 18 (still a few years away, but I'm a planner!) volunteered to fight in His Majesty's Royal Navy, along with our friend Frank. With America determined to stay out of the war, it was the least they could do, they'd told me.

Oh, how I missed them all. Those happy days on deck, all together… before everything got so messy and I had no idea what was happening anymore. Ever since the war began in Europe, it was as though someone had taken the world, stuffed it in a jar, and shaken it very hard, leaving us all barely knowing what was up and what was down. This feeling, a vague loneliness and longing for *something* familiar, was only amplified by the pipes.

Glancing at my bed-side clock, I groaned. It was already 8:45am! How had I slept in so much? Was it possible I was still growing? I was tall enough! Mrs. Butterfield hated tardiness at breakfast almost as much as she hated the Nazis. And she hated the Nazis.

As I did every morning, I reached for my little

pocket Bible and opened up to where I'd left off the day before. 1 Peter 4:10-11; *"Each of you should use whatever gift you have received to serve others, as faithful stewards of God's grace in its various forms."* It was a short and sweet reading today, and that was a blessing because I was late.

Quickly, I pushed back the blue and white chenille blanket and stood up, walking to the window. I splashed water on my face from the small bowl on my washstand and began to brush my hair (cut in a sharp bob), looking out at the green lawn and the even rows of boys all in the middle of pushups. In the back row, I saw Horatio in his white shorts, white t-shirt, and white tennis shoes, my father in his all-American blue jeans, and Ferguson in his uniform (albeit, without his jacket). All three had taken to joining the boys for morning exercises. The tutors were all too old to be of much use in that department!

A quick glance in the mirror showed I had not changed since the night before. Tall. Hair tucked behind my ears. Eyes, large and thoughtful, more thoughtful than the summer before!

I checked the clock again. I had five minutes to get to the kitchen and avoid the wrath of Mrs. Butterfield!

* * *

"Agatha!" Mrs. Butterfield called. She refused to call me by my nickname, Piper, saying, "I'll not go using a name God did not give you, Agatha Gordan." I wanted to protest that my parents had given me the name Agatha, and even *they* called me Piper, but she would have none of it. She had a commanding, domineering presence, and her word, in the kitchen, was law. So in the kitchen I was Agatha.

I stood next to her large motherly form near the stove and received a bowl of oats and looked as penitent as I could.

"What have I told you about breakfast?"

"You don't serve after 9:00 in the morning."

"And what time is it?" she asked, looking at me with a sharp stare.

I glanced at my watch. It was 9:02. So close.

"I'm sorry. It won't happen again, Mrs. Butterfield."

She made a "tsk tsk tsk" sound with her teeth and peered down at me sideways. "Don't make promises you can't keep, Agatha Gordan. How am I supposed to feed you, your family, and dozens of school boys if you are tardy? It wrecks the whole system!"

I was about to say that two minutes couldn't have made much of a difference, but wisely held my tongue. Truth be told, even with the older boys rotating to help with dish duty, manning the kitchen duties of the estate was an unpleasant, thankless, never-ending job.

One could not win with a woman like Mrs. Butterfield. *At least*, I thought to myself as I tasted the oats topped with heavy cream, *she's a good cook*. She'd added dried pears and vanilla into the porridge. It was very difficult to get sugar these days with the rationing. And the pears added a lovely sweetness and flavor.

There sat my mother and Edie at the old long pine kitchen table, drinking coffee and reading their papers of choice. Despite being on strict bedrest, Edie refused to eat upstairs. My mother read the *New York Times*, and my aunt, *The Scotsman* (the paper I worked for). By the looks of things, my mother was looking at the sports section. I could tell because her serious brown eyes looked even more serious, though not sad, which is how she looked when she read the news. The sports trend was a funny trait she'd taken on since coming to Scotland. She said knowing the status of American baseball made her feel better about the status of the world. Anna sat next to my aunt in a special wooden chair that was higher than the others, pretending to read the funnies. She was dressed in a miniature version of the bathrobe Edie wore. My mother had sewn both.

Beside Anna was Fanny, the little monkey we'd picked up in Morocco the summer before. She wore a tiny red sweater knitted by my mother to keep her comfortable in the constant chill of Northern Scotland. My mother was, unlike me, very good at crafty things like knitting and sewing.

"Look at this!" Edie exclaimed, one freckled hand on her belly, the other holding up the paper covering her face so I could only see her forehead and a strip of her thick auburn hair pulled back into a French braid. There, dead and center, was the picture of the giant sheep with the words *"Scotland's Wooliest Sheep, 'Beefcake,' Wins County Prize!"* written boldly above it.

"It's a very good picture, dear. Very . . . clear. You can really make out how enormous the fellow is. Not your best work, but it has the air of a professional about it!"

I crossed my eyes and stuck a spoonful of oats into my mouth and groaned. "If only I had more interesting subjects to work with, I might get somewhere!"

Edie sighed and nodded her head as she put the paper back on the table. With a dramatic fluttering of her eyelashes, she exhaled loudly. "Fighting in Ethiopia between the Italians and the Belgian Congolese has stopped for the rainy season. And the Luftwaffe has tried to bomb the Rolls Royce engine factory in the East Midlands in England. Miraculously, the bombs only killed a few animals nearby. But when will this madness end?"

At this, I saw my mother's eyes peeked out from behind her own paper. She looked disappointed.

"Dodgers lose?"

My mother sighed heavily and went back to reading.

I ate my oatmeal in silence for a minute or two, watching as my mother and aunt turned the pages of their respective papers. Suddenly, a fist knocked sharply three times on the kitchen window just above the sink. The window was about six-feet from the ground, and whoever was knocking was shorter than that, so all we could see was the hand.

"Who could that be?" Mrs. Butterfield dried her hands on her apron and went to the kitchen door and opened it.

"Hello?" A feminine voice sounded from outside.

"What do you want, miss?" Mrs. Butterfield asked briskly.

A face appeared in the door. It belonged to a tall, thin woman, wearing thick glasses, her hair covered by a kerchief. She was dirty and tired and looked as though she had been walking all night. A simple brown suit hung on her thin frame. It was cheaply made and fit her badly.

"I'm so sorry I'm barging in like this." The woman smiled wearily, revealing an adorable gap between her two front teeth. "I'm trying to get back to Kingsbarns but got totally turned around, and now I have no idea where I am. Even this place is confusing." She looked at us apologetically. "I couldn't even find the front door!"

"Happens all the time." My aunt smiled. "It's my husband's house, well, it's an estate, really. Belonged to his family for generations. You can blame them. No sense of congruity at all, but plenty of romance."

The original medieval castle, with a great wall and a tower and ramparts built along a cliff that plunged into the freezing sea below, stood through the late 18th century, until it crumbled beyond repair. Uncle Horatio's grandfather built the "new house," a Gothic revival style mansion right up against the ruins. The old and the new, the brick turrets and stone walls on the edge of the sea were a mess of architecture and reflected the eccentricities of the generations of owners. Thankfully, Horatio had the whole thing wired for electricity before we'd moved in. But it is still a cold house. And musty because of the moisture from the sea. And there are more mice than I care to mention.

"I've never seen another one like it," the woman agreed, taking off her glasses and cleaning them on her sleeve. Dark circles rimmed her eyes, and they were red, as though she'd been crying. She leaned weakly against the counter as my aunt and mother shared a worried glance. Immediately, my aunt sprung into hostess mode. "Mrs. Butterfield, please get Mrs.—?"

"Golda," the woman swallowed, "Golda Meyerson,"

"Please get Mrs. Meyerson some tea." She pointed to the seat across from me. "Sit, won't you?"

The woman paused a moment. "Well, all right. Thank you. And it's *Miss* Meyerson."

"Miss Golda Meyerson? Well," my mother stood up and pulled out the chair, "it's nice to see another good Jewish girl in these parts."

"You too?" Golda's mouth opened in surprise. "I didn't know there were any in Scotland."

"A few. More now with the refugees from Germany. Mostly in the big cities. Up here there aren't many of anybody. Just sheep." She extended her hand and shook Golda's warmly. "I'm Rose."

"Do I detect a German accent?" Miss Meyerson tilted her head to the side.

"A very slight German accent. You have a good ear. I lived in the States much longer than I ever lived in Germany. Most people don't notice it."

"I've always been good with music and imitations and things," Golda sighed, "ever since I was a little girl."

As she sat down, my aunt leaned forward. "You know, you look familiar. I thought all the shepherdesses left for the factories in the south."

"Oh, dear me, no." She laughed slightly.

"Do I detect an *American* accent?" my mother asked as Golda accepted a cup of tea from the cook.

Golda wrapped her fingers around the cup and lifted it to her mouth, the steam fogging up her glasses. She nodded. "Philadelphia, born and raised. This is my first time in Scotland."

"Goodness," my aunt's brows knitted together. "I was sure I'd seen you before. Your eyes are so . . . so . . . what's the word? It's like deja vu or something."

"I just have one of those faces." The woman's eyes didn't leave her teacup. Then her lashes fluttered shut before opening just slightly. She seemed unwell, though more in spirit than in body.

"Don't you think she looks familiar, Rose?" Edie turned to my mother, who didn't answer but instead asked, "Miss Meyerson, what are you doing here? There are very few tourists in these parts these days."

"I was. . ." She inhaled and frowned, carefully choosing her words. "I came for a job. But things didn't work out the way I thought they would. This morning when I woke up, I didn't know what to do, so I just went walking. I heard about the heather and the cliffs and everything. I thought I ought to see them for myself."

"I completely understand." Edie nodded. "Walking helps clear the brain."

"I don't know if it cleared mine. I *still* don't know what to do." She sighed and shrugged, putting her teacup down.

"Breakfast still hot?" My father, Nathan Gordon, appeared in the kitchen doorway and marched to Mrs. Butterfield's side.

"Mr. Gordon!" Mrs. Butterfield protested. "Tempes Fugit!"

He ignored her and began to serve himself. "I've got to move quickly. I'm running late, and the clinic opens in five minutes."

He stopped short when he saw Golda. "Who's this?"

2

Miss Meyerson of Philadelphia

"*This* is Miss Meyerson of Philadelphia," my aunt said.

"I'd stay and chat, Miss Meyerson," my father, distracted as usual, crammed a large spoon of oatmeal into his mouth and continued, "but I'm late as it is, a dreadful family trait." Dad pecked my cheek and then my mother's before he disappeared out the door. At this, Mrs. Butterfield rolled her eyes.

"I hope he's not planning on running the clinic today in that get-up." Shaking her head sadly, my mother's lips turned down. "He looks like he never left the college football team."

"The boys don't care if their doctor and part-time science teacher wears blue jeans! They probably find it rather exotic. Their cowboy-doctor from California."

My aunt looked to Golda for support. "Don't you think so?"

Before she could answer, my mother continued, "I'm not worried about them. It's me. I like my husband looking like an adult." The moment she said it, the sound of a thundering herd of elephants jogging past the kitchen door and down the corridor whizzed past us. It was the boys, in lines, two by two.

Startled, Golda stood abruptly and watched wide-eyed as the parade trooped passed. Morning exercises were over, apparently. I counted the boys to myself, *two, four, six. . . sixteen. . . thirty. . . thirty-six. . . Willem and Raffi, forty. . . forty-two. . . ah, the two stragglers, Ferguson and Horatio.*

"They live upstairs," my mother explained, not going into the details.

Golda nodded as though this was the most normal thing in the world before glancing at the stack of dishes. Her eyes suddenly lit up as though she'd been struck with a great epiphany. "You wouldn't happen to be looking for help, would you?"

"Looking for help?" My mother laughed over the noise. "Under every rock and behind every door. But the help is gone. It's been gone since last September. Poof! Up in smoke with Hitler's *Blitzkrieg.*"[1]

"You know," Golda glanced nervously at Edie, "I'm

free for the foreseeable future."

"Rose, that husband of yours quit early. He cheats!" It was the boom of Horatio's booming Scottish brogue as he entered the kitchen. He was sweating a bit. He stopped at the kitchen door, clutched his side, heaving, red in the face.

"He doesn't cheat. He just goes to work in the morning."

"I'd have joined you and stayed till the last jumping jack," Edie looked down at her belly, "but you know Nathan has put me on a very strict regime of doing nothing at all. It's remarkably difficult to follow, trust me!"

At that moment, the telephone began to ring in the hall. "Get that, won't you Ferguson?" Horatio sniffed and turned his attention to the newcomer.

Instantly, Golda curtsied, knowing instinctively that this was the "lord of the manor."

"This is Miss Meyerson." Edie enunciated very clearly. Lowering her voice, she whispered, "She's looking for a job."

"A job doing what?" He frowned.

"Cleaning. Cooking. Laundry. Anything!" Golda looked down. "I *need* work."

Mrs. Butterfield turned around sharply. "Hire her! I beg you, Mr. Macleay. Before we drown in dishes."

"I second Mrs. Butterfield," my mother threw in for good measure.

"That's Ferguson's department." He put his hand over his mouth and shouted, "Ferguson!"

Ferguson's head appeared in the doorway. "Telephone's for," he faltered, looking at Golda Meyerson and then back to me, "Miss—"

"For me?" I blinked.

Ferguson shook his head in a way that was difficult to read.

Golda lowered her eyes. "I'm looking for work. I'm an experienced housemaid. I've spent several years in service."

"Is it Peter?" I asked, still unsure it was for me. My words fell on deaf ears. He was totally focused on the newcomer.

Ferguson frowned. "Have you a letter of recommendation?"

She shook her head at the butler. "Not with me." Digging into her little worn out purse, she pulled out an American passport. "Here," she said.

He looked it over. "Golda Meyerson. Residence in Pasadena, California,"

"Ferguson, is it Peter? Is he home on some surprise leave or something?" I interjected.

Ferguson didn't answer. He and Golda were,

apparently, the only people in the room, not seeing or hearing anyone but each other. It was awkward, to say the least.

"I used to work there," Golda said.

Ferguson's gaze traveled back to the passport. "Born September 8, 1904?"

"In Philadelphia."

Ferguson stared at the passport a moment more as Golda shifted her weight nervously.

"She has an honest face, Ferguson!" Edie exclaimed.

"I suppose I see nothing out of the ordinary." He sniffed and gave her the passport back. "Where are you staying, Miss Meyerson? Shall we send for your things?"

"I've nothing," she answered quickly. "My trunk was lost on the trip here."

"I see." Ferguson pursed his lips. "We'll just have to find something suitable for you to wear."

"Ferguson," I interrupted, "who's on the telephone?"

Slightly startled, he shook himself out of the strange daze and answered, "It's your editor."

"Strange. Angus never calls. He always sends a telegram. It's cheaper." I stood up and brushed off my disappointment, excusing myself with, "Duty calls."

"I say she's hired," Edie said with an air of finality as I left the room. "On probation, of course. Two weeks trial."

"If you say so, Mrs. Macleay." Ferguson sounded concerned.

"I certainly *do* say so. If the job suits Golda, that is."

"The job suits me just fine! You won't be sorry—you have no idea what it means to me. This morning I woke up, and I didn't know what to do with the rest of my life. Now? I feel like I can breathe again!" The woman's voice carried a fresh youthfulness and joy.

"Well, you haven't met the boys yet." My mother's voice drifted down the hall. "You might decide it's the end of your life."

As I jogged down the corridor to the telephone on the hall table (there were two in the house, one in the hall and one in Uncle Horatio's office), I could hear the sound of the boys in one of the classrooms upstairs doing their times tables. "Two times two is four. Four times four is sixteen," and on and on.

Pausing at the gilded table where the receiver rested on its side, I squared my shoulders and put on my most professional and mature voice. "Hello, Angus," I greeted him. (The editor of the Scotsman was not keen on last names.)

"Piper, I've got a job for you." His voice came through the line with quite a bit of static.

"Another cow born with an extra tail?" I asked.

He laughed. "Nothing like that. An exclusive! Lois Lavigne is in Kingsbarns."

My first real assignment! The sheep photograph must have really won him over!

"Lois Lavigne?" I plugged my free ear to drown out the students. "The actress?"

"No. Lois Lavigne, the deep-sea diver," he replied dryly. "Of course Lois Lavigne the actress!"

"What's she doing here?"

"Came out to shoot a movie and decided to stay for a short vacation before returning to the States. She's staying at the Crowne Pub and Inn, and she knows your coming. Got a tip she was there and set the whole thing up, an exclusive photo shoot. We'll call it 'Lois Lavigne, Abroad in the Highlands.'" I could picture Angus behind his great desk covered with stacks of articles.

I felt my hand shake a bit. "Really?"

"Full double-page spread."

"When is she expecting me?"

"Noon." With that, Angus told me to give his regards to Edie and Horatio and hung up with a clang.

Fingers tingling with excitement, I ran back to the

kitchen and nearly shouted, "I am going to take a photograph of Lois Lavigne!"

Edie's eyes opened wide and her lips parted in shock. "Lois Lavigne? In Kingsbarns?"

"She's on vacation," I said breathlessly, "and I'm to meet her at noon at the Crowne Pub and Inn!"

When I looked at Edie, she was somewhere else. "Raised in Paris," she sighed, "in one of those lovely gilded apartments. Descended from Napoleon Bonaparte. Taught to dance by none other than Jose Javier!"

"Never heard of him." My mother smiled flatly.

"He is a very famous choreographer with the Paris Opera. And we all know what *that* means!"

"Don't we." The flat note to my mother's tone betrayed her feelings towards the topic at hand. It was a well-known fact that my mother and Edie did not see eye to eye on entertainment, though their regard for one another in every other respect was well established, and they considered themselves close friends. My mother preferred reading to the movies, and though Edie was a writer, she preferred the cinema to reading. Edie had seen every film ever made (at least it seemed that way) and knew just about everything there was to know about stars and the lifestyles of the rich and famous. It was a strange hobby that irked my mother and entertained the rest of us.

It was then I noticed that the kitchen had cleared out. "Where'd everyone go?"

"Ferguson is finding Miss Meyerson a new outfit, and Horatio went to bathe after his calisthenics." My mother stood up and picked Anna up out of her chair. Gently, she took Fanny the monkey and handed her to me. "Take her back to her cage, won't you, dear?"

"I wish I could go," Edie stood up slowly. "I've always wanted to meet Lois. I've read a bit about her. She is quite self-made. Determined to make her own way in the world.." Edie looked up with a satisfied expression. "I like that in a woman."

"Let me guess," my mother paused and took a pose, "Lois travelled to New York as a young woman to work as a model. It wasn't long before she was discovered and was given an itty-bitty part in an itty-bitty picture. But during rehearsal one day, her dancing and singing talents were discovered, and a star was born! And now she is in great big pictures."

"Why," my aunt looked surprised, "yes. That's it almost exactly!"

"How do you know that, Mom?" I asked. These sorts of gossipy details were quite out of character for my mother.

"I didn't. All those people have the same backstories." She sniffed. "Now, Piper, take Anna upstairs and finish your trigonometry homework."

"I have to get ready to meet Lois!"

"Trigonometry homework," she commanded. "And I need you to take Anna with you. I can't watch her this afternoon. I'm waxing the dining room floor, and I can't have her underfoot." She said matter-of-factly.

"Mother!" I paused. "How can you expect me to have my first real assignment with a three-year-old in the room?"

"You'll just have to make do. But I expect you'll make out just fine." She winked at me. "Better go finish that trigonometry or you won't have any first assignment at all!"

With a huff, I took Anna's hand in the one that wasn't holding the monkey.

"To think," Edie murmured, "an exclusive! I'd go too, to guide you along, but your father won't let me stand for more than thirty seconds at a time." She reached out and was about to clasp my hand until she realized they were full and said emphatically, "No, you must go and represent the family. And you just *must* invite her to dinner! I've the greatest appreciation for talent like Miss Lavigne's. And I'm sure she could use some cultured company in a village of such…"

"Peasants?" my mother shouted from the hall.

"I was going to say *villagers*." She straightened her skirt and tilted her chin. "And I have nothing against small-town folk, it's just that they know next to nothing about show business in this part of the country, and I'm sure she is desperate for some comfortable conversation! We *must* have Piper extend an invitation to have dinner with us." Edie looked at my mother.

At that moment, Ferguson and Golda reappeared. She was dressed in a maid's uniform that Ferguson had found hanging in one of the old servant's quarter's closets. It looked like it had been made in 1922, but it was in fair enough shape and was only a few inches too short.

"I suppose that will do," Edie frowned, "for now."

Golda looked gleeful, as though she had been given the moon. "It's fine!"

"What room shall she stay in, ma'am? I was thinking the one across from Piper. The servant's quarters still haven't been remodeled."

"Fine, fine." Edie waved her hand and smiled contentedly. "And your first job, Golda, will be to help me get upstairs to my bedroom. I'm as big as a whale, and my balance is just about as good."

"With pleasure, Mrs. Macleay."

"Ferguson, can you take me into town this afternoon? I've got an appointment," I smiled broadly, "and you'll never guess with whom!"

"*Whom?*" Ferguson asked.

"Lois Lavigne!"

As I said it, Golda, who had one hand around Edie's waist and was helping her out of the room, tripped. "Oh my!" She laughed. "Lois Lavigne? In these parts?"

"Oh, my dear girl," Edie shook her head sadly, "many a woman who might find other places more interesting finds herself in Kingsbarns, whether she likes it or not. We all have a Kingsbarns in our life."

"Don't I know it." Ferguson muttered and turned back to me. "I can drive you into town, but you'll have to walk back. I'm doing bomb shelter inspections this afternoon and have to pick up something from the train station for your uncle"

"Inspections?" Golda asked as she helped Edie plod forward.

"I'm the air-warden for the county, ma'am."

"My," she glanced over her shoulder, "you must be busy!"

"That's why we are so grateful to have you on board, dear girl!" Edie's voice rang out. "Especially with Lois coming to dinner. You will make a perfect addition to the staff, I'm sure. Such an honest face."

3

Miss Lois Lavigne of Pasadena

Just between us, my trigonometry homework was not *exactly* finished by the time Ferguson dropped Anna and I off at the entrance to the Crowne Pub and Inn.

"Don't you wish you could come, Ferguson?" I said, pausing at the driver's door. "Meet a great actress?"

"Goodness!" Ferguson chuckled. "Miss Lois Lavigne, pretty as she may be, is not a great actress."

"Well, she's very famous. That's something exciting, don't you think?"

"Just because one is famous doesn't make one worth meeting, Miss Piper. Not when there are more important things afoot. Things like war."

"Edie says that the dancing and singing people like Lois do is important because it brings joy to people," I protested, feeling upset that Ferguson was, in his special way, belittling my first real assignment that had nothing to do with sheep.

"I've served princes and diplomats and statesmen in my work with your uncle, Miss Piper. . ."

"Everyone thinks she is so talented!" I was surprised. I knew Ferguson to be a no-nonsense sort of person. His life was his work. But to be so completely unexcited, almost annoyed, with the arrival of the star was a rare glimpse into his inner life.

"I think it's wrong to be impressed with anyone because they have mere fame, and, just between us, I find her acting to be something other than talent."

I blinked twice.

"She is a pretty face on a screen."

"Well, now I know how you feel about the movies." I felt the excitement slowly draining from the moment.

"Character, Miss Piper, is what I was taught to be impressed with. Someone always willing to lend a helping hand. Someone who prefers to serve rather than be served. And from what I can tell, that is most definitely not Lois Lavigne. Now," he reached behind the seat and pulled out an umbrella. "Take this. It looks like you'll have a spot of rain on your walk home. I truly am sorry I won't be able to pick you up."

"Don't worry about it, Ferguson." I glanced up at the darkening sky. "Anna and I could both stand a long walk today, couldn't we, Anna? And it won't rain on us! It's much too much of a good day."

The little girl nodded solemnly. Anna rarely spoke.

"Take it anyway or your mother would never forgive me." He pressed the umbrella into my hand, adjusted his driver's cap before driving away.

I watched him for a moment. And then I reached down for Anna's hand and marched into the lobby of the Crowne, my camera bag slung over my shoulder.

Entering the lobby, I saw a sight I never expected to see. There were *people*. And lots of them. By the looks of things, the whole of Kingsbarns had emerged to catch a glimpse of the famous Lois.

"Oh my goodness!" a distraught-looking matron said to her equally elderly companion in a Scottish accent so strong, it was difficult to follow what she was saying. "I've been waiting three hours for her to come down those stairs. You'd think she'd be a little more sociable, coming all this way!"

"She's here to rest, remember?" the man said.

"I don't see any reason for her to be rude, no

matter how she's feeling. I subscribe to her fan magazine! Least she could do is sign it."

The crowd in the little shabby lobby was similarly unhappy. They'd come for some entertainment and had gotten nothing at all. I pushed through a circle of gray-haired farmers smoking pipes to the front desk. Behind it, a small man with oiled black hair looked past me at the horde of fans. He was overwhelmed.

"I've come to see Miss Lois Lavigne," I said as professionally as I could.

"Hasn't everyone?" he huffed.

"I don't understand." I paused. "How did all these people find out she's here?"

"Ever heard of a party-line?"

"What?"

"The telephone line between the post office and the Macleay Manor are shared lines. The editor at the Scotsman called and let the cat out of the bag. It took less than an hour for the news to spread around the entire county. But she's not coming down. Not for anybody."

I groaned and crossed my eyes. "Well, I actually have an appointment with her." I held up my camera bag.

"You're the Girl Reporter from *The Scotsman?*"

I nodded.

"Oh," he frowned, "then you are the one who is responsible for this mayhem."

I could have argued that I had absolutely nothing to do with Lois coming to the village, but I held my tongue and instead said, "You'll ring her room and let her know I'm here?"

"Won't make a difference."

"What?"

"I have a note from Miss Lavigne's secretary. She won't be able to come down."

"What do you mean?" I stumbled over my words.

"I mean," he licked his fingers and ran them through his oily hair, "she won't come down."

"Perhaps you could ring her room?"

Before he could answer, a commotion in the back of the lobby took his attention and he stepped from behind the counter, begging a "Mrs. Walten" to stop helping herself to the mints. They were for *guests*.

"Well, Anna," I glanced down at the quiet little girl, "if she won't come down, we'll go up."

Before the man could see, we ran up the stairs and down the hall of the small inn. There were five guest rooms in all. One had four beautiful bouquets leaning up against it. "I vote that's it, don't you?"

Anna nodded, and off we marched. Cautiously, I raised my hand to knock.

"Oh, thank goodness!" a woman's voice said as the door opened. "You're back!" The minute the woman saw me (and then Anna) her face fell.

"Miss Lavigne?" I asked, thinking how different she looked than in pictures. . . how much older. . . and rounder.

The woman shook her head, and her eyes narrowed. "No. Miss Lavigne is, uh, indisposed. I'm her personal secretary."

I glanced past her into the empty room. "I had an appointment with her. I'm the Girl Reporter for *The Scotsman*. And this," I held up Anna's hand, "is my assistant. My editor set up an exclusive."

One of the woman's eyebrows went up skeptically. "Hiring rather young these days, aren't they? War shortage?"

"Where is Miss Lavigne?" I asked. "I could reschedule the interview for whenever would be most convenient."

She tried to shut the door as I tried to look behind her. "Please don't!" the woman said nervously. "Miss Lavigne is very particular about her beauty sleep."

I frowned. I had seen the room. No one was in bed. The room was empty, save for the jittery personal assistant.

"Could you let her know that we came by?"

Without answering, the door slammed in my face, leaving Anna and me alone in the hall.

"I guess we'll just walk back then," I sighed, "won't we, Anna?"

As if on cue, a great blast of thunder shook the entire inn. "Oh, perfect," I groaned. Everything had gone according to plan, I thought cynically. And to think, once I got back home, I'd still have to finish my trigonometry (unbeknownst to my mother). It would be a perfect end to a perfect day.

Back in the lobby, we inched through the crowd, and I waved down the front-desk man.

"When Lois does show up," I reached into my pocket and pulled out Edie's invitation for Lois to come to a formal dinner the next night at the manor. "Would you give her this?"

"I can give it to her secretary. Miss Lois doesn't speak to anyone," he said knowingly. "I only saw her back when she came in last night. Very mysterious woman, if you ask me."

"And her secretary?"

"She guards that room like a police chief!"

Once again, a blast of thunder shook the building. Grimacing, I pulled Anna to the door, buttoned up her sweater and then mine, opened up the umbrella, and plunged into the storm for the two-mile walk back home.

When we finally arrived, wet to the skin and mud up to our ankles, Anna was cranky and so was I. Along with a gust of wind, we blew through the front door and found my mother and Golda both on their knees, polishing the inlaid wood with lambswool tied around their knees for extra cushioning.

"Oh, good!" my mother said without looking up. "You're back. Your aunt's going nuts with this idea of Lois Lavigne coming to dinner tomorrow night. Did you get the picture? How'd the interview go?"

"Rose!" Edie's voice shouted from upstairs.

"What is it, Edie?"

"I want to serve a classic lobster boil, corn on the cob, potatoes, Mrs. Butterfield's rolls, the works! Maine classic all the way."

Mom shook her head. "Mrs. Butterfield said no corn. Potatoes, yes."

"Oh, have it your way!" Edie responded, her voice muffled by the distance. "I'm so nervous just sitting here like this. I could help you know. I could—"

"Oh no you don't!" my mother shouted up the stairs. "You aren't helping with anything until that baby shows up. Understood?"

"Rose Gordan, you are as hard-hearted as that husband of yours."

My mother rolled her eyes and ran a hand through her hair. "She's micromanaging like the queen is coming to dinner."

"I don't think she's coming," I said bluntly.

"What do you mean?" Lois stopped polishing and looked up at a suit of armor.

"She wouldn't see me. To be honest, I don't think she was there. I left the invitation at the front desk."

At that point, Mrs. Butterfield appeared, a stack of my aunt's good china in her arms. "Dear me!" She held the plates carefully. "You are both dripping wet! Go upstairs and get dry before you catch colds."

"She's right, you know." My mother nodded. "And then come back and help us, won't you?"

"But if Lois isn't coming—" I protested.

"You've finished your homework, so your afternoon should be completely free, right?" Her eyes met mine with a twinkle.

My mother had a third sense about my homework.

"What do you mean, 'she isn't coming?'" Edie called from the top of the stairs.

"Get back in bed, Edith!" My mother shook her head.

"I left the invitation at the front desk. . ." I passed Anna's hand to my mother's.

"Ye of little faith, Piper dear. She's coming! Call it women's intuition or whatever you like. But I just have this feeling we have to be prepared!"

* * *

"Where is Ferguson going," Golda asked as the butler marched by the dining room where she and I were arranging heaps of heather into bouquets for the table. My aunt was determined that when Lois Lavigne arrived, we would welcome her like the Hollywood royalty she was. "He only just got back from his bomb shelter inspection."

I went to the window and watched as Ferguson steadily walked down the lane to Kingsbarns. Pulling the blackout curtains back together, I checked my watch. It was only 4:30, but Ferguson preferred we have the house blacked out long before the sun set. All afternoon I'd been dreading calling Angus. I couldn't imagine what he might say when he found out Lois had stood me up. My first exclusive. Gone. Just like that. It was terribly disappointing.

"He's the warden for the village," I answered, only half-concentrating on Golda's question. "And he takes his job very seriously. Sounding sirens, guiding people to air-raid shelters, issuing and checking gas masks, that sort of thing."

Golda sighed with a hint of wistfulness. "He's lucky. You all are, you know?"

I looked back at Golda, whose eyes were locked on her arrangement. In the afternoon we'd spent dusting, shining, and mopping, I'd found her to be a very pleasant woman, if a little strange. She had no possessions of any kind, save her purse. She had a girl-next-door quality—familiar, pretty. In fact, she might have been considered stunning if not for the dark circles under her eyes. The fact that she wore glasses and had a distinct gap in her teeth made her even prettier. My mother taught me that it is our imperfections that make us real and approachable. That was Golda. Imperfect, approachable, and with every passing minute happier and more talkative.

"You have an interesting accent, Golda," I said. "It sounds very refined. Like Katherine Hepburn or someone like that."

"It's called a Transatlantic accent, and my mother worked very hard to make sure I had one. She was quite strict. Filled my mouth with marbles and all other sorts of tortures. She was in the theater when she was younger. Wanted the same for me. Sometimes I think I should have listened!"

"Vaudeville?"

She paused a moment. "Not exactly."

It took her just a split second too long to answer questions that caught her off guard, as though she didn't know how much, if anything, to share. But she was very helpful, kind, and, to be honest, rather wonderful to have around. Anna took to her immediately, following her this way and that. Golda was everywhere, helping with everything and everyone. She threw herself into the job like her life depended on it. Even now, as we arranged the flowers, it was with a quiet gusto.

"He's a very dedicated man, isn't he?" she said quietly, drawing the conversation back to Ferguson.

I nodded.

"And handsome too."

"Ferguson?" I looked again out the window. I'd never really thought of Ferguson as handsome, but then, I'd never really thought of his looks at all.

"Classic aquiline nose. That dark hair. Good voice. He'd do great in Hollywood."

I turned around and watched her from behind as she began another arrangement. "I'm happy he's not there," she went on, "because he's much better off here."

"Why would you say that?" I looked at her quizzically.

Her hands froze. "He seems like a real person, that's all. Hollywood chews up real people until they are something else altogether, and then it spits them out and no one knows who they are anymore, even themselves."

Just when I was about to ask how she knew so much about what Hollywood did to people, she blurted out, "Is he single?"

"Ferguson? Single? Why," I laughed, "that's almost as funny as thinking he's handsome."

She turned on her heel and pointed a sprig of heather at my face. "Honey, by the time you reach the fine old age of thirty-six, handsomeness takes on a whole new meaning. And trust me, Ferguson, from the top of his air-raid helmet to the soles of his faithfully and immaculately polished shoes, is the definition of an attractive man."

"If you say so." I laughed and returned to the table.

"Have you seen much action?" she went on. She'd been talking like this all afternoon, like she had a well of pent-up words. It didn't bother me in the least either. Thirty-six she may have been, but she treated me as her peer. My friendship tank, long running on empty, began to fill.

"Action?"

"Bombing I mean," she deftly moved a flower to the right. She had a very good eye.

"Oh, heavens, no." I pulled out the starched napkins from under the grand buffet against the far wall. "Why would the Nazis want to bomb a place like Kingsbarns?"

"Still," Golda sighed again, "I envy him. Getting to really do something to protect people against the Germans. All of you actually!"

"Why would you envy us?"

"You are all doing your part!" she blurted out, blushing a little. "I would do anything to be useful."

"And you are!" a voice said. My mother and Mrs. Butterfield entered from the hall that led to the kitchen.

"In fact," it was Mrs. Butterfield speaking, "I don't know how we've gotten on so long without you. I saw those potatoes you peeled, dear. Like a true professional!" (Coming from Mrs. Butterfield, this was high praise indeed.)

"I've peeled my fair share of potatoes." She smiled proudly. "But thanks just the same. You have no idea how it feels to have people think I'm helpful, to help with what matters."

"Peeling potatoes matters?" I asked, one eyebrow raised.

"It's feeding people. A few dozen little boy refugees from London. And that is important, isn't it?" From underneath the playful tone there was an underlying anxiety, as though she desperately needed her work to matter. But I was the only one who noticed it.

"Now," Mrs. Butterfield sat down at the table. "you'd think with Horatio being the lobster king of the Atlantic ocean, I could get a decent bushel full, but Sam (the grocer boy) said the catch last night was rather bad and brought me two chickens instead. For the record, they are going to cost your aunt and uncle the next two months meat rations."

"Oh no!" Golda blanched.

"What?" Mrs. Butterfield balked, "You think she'd prefer the lobster?"

Golda swallowed. "No, she won't. To be honest, I, uh, I think she's a vegetarian."

"A vegetarian?" My mother picked up Anna and set her on the polished table.

"How would you know that?" I asked.

"I. . . I read it in a fan magazine."

At this, my mother also sat down wearily. "Well, that works out just fine. We essentially only eat vegetables these days. Besides, she might not even come."

"You never know." Golda shrugged. "Stranger things have happened. But regardless, Mrs. Butterfield, save the chickens for children. I'm sure she'd prefer it went to them."

"What do you think the odds are that Lois actually comes?" I asked.

Mrs. Butterfield, Golda, and my mother stared at me blankly.

Frowning, I exhaled. "That's what I thought too. I guess I better call my editor. I hope he doesn't fire me."

4

The Missing Movie Star

"Why," Horatio bellowed cheerfully as Golda served the expertly peeled potatoes alongside individual Lord Woolton Pies (a strange wartime creation of cauliflower, parsnips, and carrots held together with a thick brown gravy seasoned with Marmite and topped with a wholemeal flour pastry made with a *tiny* bit of rendered beef fat), "what do you think, Miss Meyerson? Will this do?"

It was 8:00 in the evening, dinner time for the family. These were quieter hours at the manor. The older boys from the school were all studying, the younger ones already in bed. Usually, we ate dinner in the formal dining room. But given how hard we'd worked on setting the grand mahogany table for Lois in the hopes she'd join us the next evening, we were forced to eat in the much humbler kitchen setting.

Golda beamed. "This is by far the most interesting establishment I've ever worked in."

Edie jovially raised her glass of lemonade. "Isn't it wonderful!"

"We're very grateful for your help. Everyone says you were simply indispensable today," Horatio commented.

"The pleasure is all mine, Mr. Macleay." She nodded her head and went on serving as though she'd done so all her life. Then she excused herself and returned to the sink and began washing up. (By now, Mrs. Butterfield had returned home to her cottage.)

"Did you get a hold of Angus?" my father asked me quietly.

"I called but he had already left the office. I'll try him again tomorrow," I said, dreading the thought of it. "You know, I might go back into town and see if I can find her. I'll get that picture if it's the last thing I do!" My determination was mounting.

"Well, Edie," Horatio spoke loudly across the table to where she sat on the opposite end. "Do you want the good news or the bad news?"

"It's not very bad, is it?" She gasped a little. "Are Peter and Frank all right?"

He shook his head no and stroked his thick black beard. "Peter and Frank are, to my knowledge, right as rain. The bad news is not 'bad,' at least by the standards of bad news these days."

Edie threw her hands up. "Well, you better still give me the good news first. It will soften the bad."

"Give me just a second." He stood up and dashed out.

"What'd he do?" my mother asked my father.

He shrugged. "Beats me. I was busy setting Edward Smyth's broken wrist all afternoon."

"Edward broke his wrist?" Edie said sadly. "Poor little boy! He's the redhead, right?"

"Ran right into a wall." My father motioned with his arms. "Smack!"

By now, Horatio had returned, pushing an enormously heavy crate on wheels nearly six feet tall.

"Oh, Horatio!" Edie exclaimed. "What did you buy?"

"*Rent*, my dear, *rent*." He stood up straight and leaned against the box. "This is a 1937 Peerless/Simplex model e-7 film projector." At this we all gasped. "And it's on its way to St. Andrews to make its final resting place in the Golden Palace Theater. But I begged old Bertie at the station to let us borrow it for the weekend. He owed me a favor."

"You didn't!" Edie exclaimed.

Horatio blushed a little. "I know how much my wife likes the flicks, and I thought we could all stand to have a little real entertainment. With sound and everything."

"Wow." My father leaned back in his chair. "Brings me right back to 1927. It will be like watching the *Jazz Singer* all over again."[1]

"What will we be watching?" I asked, wide-eyed. I couldn't believe how excited I was. Going to the movies used to be such a basic thing, like going to a football game or running downtown for ice cream. Come to think of it, it had been nearly a year since I'd done anything normal like that!

"Oh ho!" he rubbed his hands together. "Nothing but the latest and the greatest. There's the big hit of last year *Gone With the Wind*. It's supposed to be very deep, very grand!"

Golda made a terrible snorting noise and drew all our attention to the sink.

"What was that, Miss Meyerson?" Horatio froze. "Is there something you want to share?"

Golda put the plate she was washing down and turned slowly to face us. "Oh dear," she said apologetically. "I didn't mean to interrupt like that. I saw it a few months ago."

"If you have something to share—" Horatio sniffed, visibly annoyed that "the help" was intruding on the family dinner conversation, "—please do."

"I just don't think that *Gone with the Wind* is either deep or grand."

Horatio blinked. "What *do* you think?"

"I think it's decadent and prejudiced. Just when filmmakers have a responsibility to make movies that matter, they make *Gone With the Wind,* and it takes home a gazillion Oscars. And for what? Glorifying American slave culture and vilifying the North." Suddenly, she took a dramatic pose, holding the sponge up in the air. As she spoke, her voice went from Golda to full-on Southern belle. "As God is my witness, as God is my witness, they're not going to lick me. I'm going to live through this, and when it's all over, I'll never be hungry again. No, nor any of my folk. If I have to lie, steal, cheat, or kill, as God is my witness, I'll never be hungry again."[2]

She stopped short and once more became Golda. "Personally, I'd rather starve to death than lie, steal, cheat or kill." Shaking her head slowly, she continued, "That's what happens when writers tell weak stories that don't matter. They hold our attention with spectacle and sparkle and special effects and scandal, but are we better for it? The characters are terrible people who do terrible things. Movies like that are hollow and not one bit true. They encourage the audience to be equally hollow and untrue. We need strong, brave, true stories. We have to, or. . . or. . ." here she swallowed, ". . .or society is bound to fail. Why, just look at Germany and the movies they make!"[3]

Coughing behind his napkin, my father scratched the side of his head and looked at Golda. "Are you saying that films like *Gone with the Wind* should be censored?"

"Oh dear me, no! I don't want to live in a country where *Gone with the Wind* couldn't be made. Rather, I want to live in a country where people are smart enough not to buy it and love it and eat it up like it was birthday cake. But that's the way of the world. Silly things sell, and money drives the world."

She paused, thinking through her words, before adding, "I think movie studios know sordid love affairs with selfish people, a smattering of prejudice, and great big fancy special effects *sell*. But spectacle alone can't hit the human heart. Good stories don't need all the glitter to capture our attention."

"What *do* they need?" Edie asked, her brows furrowed.

Golda shrugged. "Money."

"Money?"

"Good stories need money," she repeated. "But no one in Hollywood wants to risk telling the truth when lies sell."

She swallowed and seemed to remember where she was. "I apologize for the interruption. I sometimes speak out of turn. Please finish your dinner. I'll be quiet." She stood there awkwardly, not looking at anyone while the whole family sat there looking at her in the ill-fitting maid's costume.

I glanced at Edie. Her eyes were shining. She stood up slowly and proclaimed, "My dear, as a writer, I feel deeply what you are saying. I am a firm believer in telling the truth, the whole truth, and nothing but the truth. As both a writer-and as an artist, it's my job to tell society the truth. Truth touches the heart and gets people emotionally involved. Honest, true art is what changes the world!"[4] She clasped her hands together dramatically and stared off into the distance, her soliloquy finished.

"Thank you, Edie, for your rousing speech." Horatio coughed again. "Now please sit down."

"But that's just it!" Golda cried. "Powerful people, like the Nazis, know that ideas can be controlled, but emotion cannot. So if they can keep people from feeling emotions, like compassion or love or even guilt for committing evil acts, they can control them."[5]

"But a true artist," Edie said solemnly, "can change things with the truth."

Golda stepped forward. "It explains why the Nazis hold such a tight grip on the arts. Nothing gets past Hitler. And what are the German people allowed to see? Stupid pastoral scenes of idealized German peasant families, statues of impossibly perfect men and women, operas and symphonies about Germany's mythic heroic past. Don't even mention jazz! It's too African. And don't mention Mendelssohn. He's too Jewish, even if he converted! And anything A-tonal is banned too! More books than I care to name are burned, including the works of Hemingway *and* Jack London!"

"No!" Edie exclaimed, horrified. "Not Jack!"

"But *Gone with the Wind* is safe, beloved even. The book and the movie were a big hit in Berlin. With its slaves singing and laughing while they pick cotton like carefree children. Maybe that's what people in Berlin think the Jews are doing in concentration camps? Singing and laughing." Her face hardened. "Hitler said the wrong side won the American Civil War. He complained, and I quote, 'The Yankee invaders took away the continent's last great hope for an Aryan paradise.' German films, which used to be a credit to their nation," Golda was beginning to sound like a professor, "have essentially picked up their skirts and followed Hitler right off a cliff like a pack of lemmings. Now German films are mostly propaganda pieces to convince the German people that Jews are taking over the world. And let's not even talk about paintings. It would take up the rest of your dinner."[6]

By now, tears were streaming down Edie's face. She clasped her hands over her heart and shook her head. "Golda Meyerson! Golda, Golda, Golda! You are a jewel! A treasure! Imagine, such a kindred spirit joining our little household. To everything you said, I say, amen, and bravo!" She paused for effect and then said. "Quite inspiring! I dare say you shouldn't be in that uniform, but on a pulpit, preaching to the masses!"

"I doubt they would listen to me." Golda regained her composure and turned to Horatio. "I do apologize again, Mr. Macleay."

"Apologize for what, dear girl?"

"I've no right to tell your family what to watch or not. I am just a servant, and I hope this little passionate outburst of mine won't get me fired. I *need* this job."

Horatio, still a little stunned, answered quickly, "No, no, no, my dear girl. No need to apologize. This is an open house. We welcome learning here, don't we boys?"

Willem and Raffi jerked their heads up and down, obviously unsure of what was happening but enjoying the commotion nevertheless.

"And we value a good philosophical discussion!" Edie lowered her chin in thankful acknowledgement.

Curtseying and nodding, Golda said quietly, "Now, if you'll excuse me, I'm going to go start on the mending. I need to, uh… collect myself."

"Mending?" my father asked as Golda disappeared.

"She said she could sew, so I gave her a basket of garments that have been worn through." Mom replied, looking at the door from where Golda had disappeared. "My, she's more excitable than I took her for."

"Excitable? I'd say the young woman's downright radical." Horatio looked towards the door.

My father looked at my mother, still thinking of the mending. "My good flannel?"

"It's in the basket," she assured him with a grin.

Willem nudged Raffi and said in heavily accented English, "How are we going to watch a movie if we can't watch *Gone with the Wind*?"

"I've a few other reels that came with the projector on their way to the theater… including the latest Lois Lavigne." Horatio chuckled, trying to loosen the strangely tense quality of the air. "It's about a country girl who inherits her estranged uncle's Paris fashion house. It's called *Lovely Lady*. I can't imagine it would offend our new maid. Pretty tame stuff. Nothing political."

"Now, Horatio," Edie braced herself and pushed her plate away, "I'm ready for the bad news."

"Yes, about that." Horatio picked up his fork and resumed eating. "Miss Lois Lavigne, according to village gossip, became very very ill with some sort of food poisoning last night and is still recovering. Odds are, she won't be coming tomorrow night."

Strange, I thought to myself. *If she was sick, why hadn't she been in bed when I visited her room at the inn?*

"Oh no! Poor girl!" Edie sighed. "Nathan, you must stop by and check in on her tomorrow. Make sure she's alright. All alone in a strange village!"

My mother glanced at me. "Piper dear, would you take Anna upstairs and put her to bed?"

I nodded and helped Anna down from her chair.

Silently, we wound our way through the great house and upstairs. I could see a light coming through Golda's door, the room right across from my own. The old servants' quarters were in dire disrepair, and no one, not even a dog (according to my aunt) could have slept in them. I stopped and listened for a moment, but no sound came from it.

"Gute Nacht!" Anna said loudly through the door.

"Who's there?" Golda called.

"Anna wants to say goodnight," I responded, pushing the door open. There was Golda sitting on the great big four-poster bed, needle in hand, diligently sewing my father's shirt. The blackout curtains were drawn tight.

"Well," she looked up, "goodnight, Miss Anna. I'll see you bright and early tomorrow morning." Then to me she added, "My, she's sweet."

"She's become almost a daughter to Edie and Horatio, and the twins like sons."

"Like an instant family."

I nodded and whispered, "No one talks about the fact they'll have to be sent back to their parents, eventually."

"I pray they have parents to go back to," she said quietly.

I looked down at the top of Anna's head.

"So what goes on here at night? Anything fun and exciting?"

"When my cousins were still here, we always did something fun. Cards, music, just sitting up talking and laughing."

"Sounds like heaven."

"But now my parents and my aunt and uncle are so tired at night, they'll all collapse into bed in about half an hour." I laughed a little.

"And you?"

"I'll try to finish my homework, I guess, though I doubt I'll make much progress."

"I could help you!" she responded eagerly. "What are you studying?"

"Trigonometry."

"Oh." Her face fell. "Well, maybe not. Just between us," she lowered her voice till it was a whisper, "I never actually graduated high school. I started working when I was 16. But I'm very good at memorizing poetry and diction. And I never stopped learning. I'm always reading something."

"I wish I could stop school and start working."

"Trust me, Piper, that's not what you want at all." She looked at me and then around the room. "This house is magnificent, you know. Really beautiful. It's having a wonderful effect on me. I haven't felt so energized in years."

Anna yawned and tugged on my hand. "I ought to get her in bed," I said, scooping her into my arms.

"Yes, of course."

As I left, I saw Golda's meager possessions, her suit

she'd worn that day and her purse, thrown over the back of a soft armchair covered in chenille.

There was clearly more to the mysterious woman's story. Much more. And I was determined to find out what it was.

5
A Question of Censorship

I t took much longer to put Anna to bed then usual. We sang three songs, and I told her two stories. As she slowly drifted off, I replayed the events at dinner. Golda had said a lot of things I didn't really understand. It left me feeling sort of nervous-excited, but I wasn't sure why. So after Anna finally fell asleep (she still refused to go to sleep alone), I stopped by my parents' room. They were both in bed reading.

"Horatio volunteered to do the dishes?" I asked, surprised.

My mother lifted her reading glasses off her nose. "Nope. Golda came down. She is an absolute Godsend."

"And smart!" my father added.

"She never graduated high school," I said, sitting on the end of the bed.

My father looked at me with a look that said, "Spill." I only came to talk to my parents late at night when I had something to get off my chest.

"I'm confused about what Golda was saying."

"How so?" My mother sat up a bit more and leaned back against the headboard.

"Should *Gone with the Wind* have been allowed to have been made, if it really romanticizes something so wrong, like slavery?" I thought of the film's premise and how the whole movie glorified the "great days of the American South."

"*Allowed* to be made?" My father looked at me. "That's not for me to say. Should people have had the common sense to not make it because it promotes ideas that hurt people? That's another question altogether." He harrumphed and looked back at his book.

My mother turned to me. "Remember how I told you about when I was a young journalism student, and I wrote articles for the school paper on racism in the South and Jim Crow laws and how they must stop if we want America to be what we say it is? Free, with equal opportunities for all, no matter your color, religion, or if you are a man or a woman?"[1]

I nodded. She'd received four anonymous, threatening letters and two menacing phone calls warning her to quit while she was ahead. She didn't pay any heed though and went right on with the series of articles. And thankfully, nothing bad happened. She repeated the story whenever she wanted me to remember not to give in to fear and to do the right thing.

"My editor," my mother inhaled, "could have been scared off by the response of those articles. But he was a firm believer that society can never be destroyed by free speech. He told me we have to believe that people will choose to see the truth and do the right thing, no matter what lies might be spread around."

"So people should be allowed to say whatever they want in the movies?" I froze.

My mother's shoulders raised a little. "The Bible is very clear that certain things should never be said or shown because it may hurt us or others."

"But what about ideas?" I pressed. "Portrayals of events in history from a perspective that is skewed? Isn't that dangerous?"

"You are venturing into murky waters, Piper dear. The freedom we cling to in order to speak the truth is the same freedom others will use to speak falsehood. Take that freedom away, and you wind up with a situation like Germany, where the only voice broadcast is the voice of an evil dictator. As it stands, we have to take the good with the bad and trust God to know what is true and what isn't. Ideally, we'll know our history well enough to sniff out deceptive stories that mislead and rewrite facts, and put them where they belong—in the garbage! Thank goodness we still can educate our children as we see fit." She put her reading glasses back on. "One way or another, *Gone with the Wind* was a massive hit, which tells you a great deal about where the American public stands and how they think and how they *want* to think. They prefer history through a rose-colored lens, ignoring the truth of what so many of their neighbors are suffering in the South right now with Jim Crow! These days, audiences prefer to eat cotton candy entertainment. Big, fluffy, sticky sweet, and about as substantial as a cloud."

"Very optimistic perspective, Rose." My father laughed without mirth.

"Just between us, there are days I'm grateful to be in Scotland." She smiled sadly, "*Especially t*hese days."

"So what do we do?" I asked, feeling a strange urgency in my gut.

"Pray that God gives us wisdom to know what's real and true and what's a lie. We can't just go to the movies without thinking."

"Don't check my brain at the door, huh?" I sighed.

"*That's* what's dangerous," she agreed. "Much more dangerous than a film like *Gone with the Wind* being made or not being made." My mother leaned forward and kissed my cheek. "But right now, all you need to do is finish your homework."

I groaned and slid off the bed. "All right."

"Don't go to bed too late."

With that, I made the long trek back to my room (on the opposite side of the house) and stared at my trigonometry textbook until my eyes began to burn. Then, still having made no progress, I slipped out of my skirt and blouse and into my nightgown and robe.

As I did so, it occurred to me that Golda had nothing to sleep in, save her slip. I had an extra nightgown *somewhere*. Oh, yes, I remembered. It was downstairs, in the basement hanging to dry.

The light was still on in Golda's room when I emerged into the hall, though the rest of the house was very quiet.

"Golda?" I knocked on the door again. "Are you still awake?"

There was no answer. Slowly, I pushed the door open. The room was empty. Odd. Maybe she was using the washroom at the end of the hall. I tiptoed to the bathroom—it was empty. Where was she?

Down the hall and the stairs I went, moving towards the kitchen and the basement, all the while listening carefully. I stopped just as I reached the library. A small table lamp was on, and Golda was hunched over the telephone on my uncle's desk. She was speaking very quietly, but forcefully enough for me to hear.

"You what? You called the police! Call them right back and tell them I was out, and now I'm back, and I'm so sick I can't see anyone. Very contagious! No wait, tell them I went back to California." This was followed by the indiscernible muttering of a frantic female voice on the other side of the line. "If they won't believe I went to California already because of the train schedule, tell them I'm leaving tomorrow night." She held her breath as the voice on the other end went on and on.

"Where am I? I'm perfectly safe. That's all you need to know. And no, I don't know when I'm coming back. Maybe I won't! And I don't care about my contract. You can go right back to Mr. 'M' in California and tell him I said so!" With that, Golda hung up the phone and crumpled into the padded leather armchair behind the desk in a tight ball, knees pulled up to her chest, and burst into tears.

Slowly, I stepped into the library. "Golda?"

Her head lifted from her knees and her eyes peered through foggy glasses into mine.

"Are you alright?"

"Fine." She brushed a tear away from her cheek. "I was just talking to. . . the railway station about my trunk."

"At midnight?"

"California time," she answered, looking as confused as I felt.

"Sure." I shuffled my feet, not sure what to say. "I thought you might want something to sleep in. I've an extra nightgown if you want. It's clean."

"I'd like that very much."

She stood up and followed me into the kitchen and through the side door that led to the basement (and where we did our laundry). Neither of us spoke.

I found the nightie hanging on the line in the basement, thrust it under my arm, and we returned upstairs. Just as we did so, Ferguson came in through the back door. He looked tired.

"Long night?" I asked.

"It's far from over." He sighed and looked from me to Golda. "I just came back to get a cup of coffee. You are both up late." Ferguson studied Golda very intently, so much so that she blushed.

Golda shrugged. "I'm used to late nights and early mornings."

"Comes with the business, doesn't it?"

"Let me make your coffee?" Her voice went up a bit.

Before he could answer, she was at the stove boiling water and rummaging through the pantry for the instant coffee.

"Strange happenings in the village." He sat down and took his helmet off. "I ran into the constable. He told me—and this stays confidential, girls—that Lois Lavigne is missing." He snapped his fingers. "Seems like the poor girl just vanished."

Golda turned her head to face the butler. "I heard she was sick."

I watched as the water boiled, and she poured it over the freeze-dried grounds and passed the cup to Ferguson. He hesitated, staring at her hand before taking the cup.

"Go to bed, Miss Meyerson," he said kindly. "I'm sure you must be tired."

"See you in the morning, sir." She curtseyed and left, leaving the butler and me all alone.

"She asked if you were single," I said when Golda was out of earshot.

"Ha!" He slapped his hand down on the table and turned deep red. "I never."

"She *is* pretty."

"Certainly," he choked. "But. . . it simply isn't done!"

"What isn't?" I asked.

"Staff seeing staff."

"Always the proper gentleman, aren't you Ferguson?"

"I know my place." He smiled sadly.

"Golda seems determined that this is her place too." I leaned back, enjoying how uncomfortable Ferguson was. But after a second, I realized that wasn't what was bothering him.

"I can't help but feel Golda is not all she seems." The embarrassed smile passed, and he frowned again. "Did you see her hands? Never done a lick of work in her life."

I thought about it. "I don't know about that. Golda seemed right at home with the dustpan. Mrs. Butterfield said she peeled potatoes like the best of them."

"I don't know what she is, Piper. It is the glory of God to conceal a matter, the glory of kings to search it out!"

"Well spoken, Ferguson." I grinned.

"Yes, well, I can only pray that whatever she's concealing won't hurt the family. I have to go, but in the meantime, find out what you can. Ask probing questions. I should hate for the family to get hurt because we failed in our duty to investigate a suspicious person. Now, you go to bed! We'll reconvene in the morning."

I stood up and saluted. "Yes, sir!"

It was then I realized I still had the nightgown in my arms.

"Oh, yes," he blinked as he remembered something, "I completely forgot. I picked this up for your aunt earlier from the drugstore. Latest *Modern Stars.*"

"For Edie?" I said fingering the gossip magazine.

"She asked me to pick it up for her."

He stood up as I opened the magazine to the front page. There, smack dab in the middle, was a picture of Lois Lavigne on the set of *All That Is Gold Does Not Glitter.* I looked at the picture closer. "Say, Ferguson," I looked up, "don't you think that Golda looks a bit like Lois?"

"I suppose there is a vague resemblance," He moved towards the door. "But of course, I wouldn't know. I don't keep up on how actresses look."

My eyes went back to the photograph. The resemblance was *strong.* On the other hand, Lois had perfect teeth. No glasses either. And Golda said she was thirty-six, not twenty-six (which is how old the magazine said Lois was underneath the photograph). But still, the resemblance, the winsome smile, the sparkling eyes.

It was like a bright neon sign was flashing in my mind, pointing to the possibility that Golda was actually. . . *Is it possible? Could Golda be—*

"And Piper!" Ferguson's voice startled my concentration. "Ask her if she's free to meet me for a walk tomorrow afternoon."

"I thought staff weren't supposed to get involved with staff!" I stifled a slight chuckle.

"Strictly business," he said, though I noted a faint blush. "I want to ask her about her previous employment. Nail down an address to send an inquiry for a character reference."

"I bet you do." I smiled.

"Wipe that smirk off that innocent face, *Agatha* Gordan. Miss Meyerson is much too pretty and refined to—"

"So!" I pointed my finger at his chest. "You admit she's pretty!"

Rolling his eyes, he gave up and smiled. "Yes, she's pretty. Very, very pretty. But don't think I'm about to drop my guard." With that, he adjusted his helmet and marched out the back door.

It was then, in the dim light of the kitchen with Lois's photograph staring back at me, that the idea hit me like an anvil. It was so simple, I scarcely believed it would work. But I had nothing to lose, did I? And so, magazine in hand, I darted upstairs and jogged back to Lois's room. It was time to put my and Ferguson's suspicions (though his were admittedly more sinister than mine) at rest.

Miss Lavigne Comes to Visit

"Golda?" I knocked softly on the door. When she didn't answer, I pushed it open. I saw her, sitting on the small chair by the dressing table, still in the silly maid's costume. She was looking in the mirror very intently and didn't see me walk up behind her.

Her hair was down, very long, and thick. She'd brushed it. Her glasses were off, folded in front of her, and her mouth shut tight. I looked down at the magazine in my hand.

The face of the movie star stared back at me. It was almost identical to the woman's face reflected in the mirror. Except that Golda looked older. She was like Lois's long lost, older twin.

I stepped closer, eyes narrowed. She was so deep in

thought; she didn't see or hear me. The whole thing was strange. Very, very strange.

It was time to put my idea to the test.

"Miss Lavigne?"

"Yes?" Golda answered unconsciously.

I dropped the magazine, and it landed with a thud. Much to my shock, the experiment was successful.

She turned and faced me, her cheeks pale, then turned back toward the mirror—seemingly emotionally untouched. We stared at each other for a moment.

"That was too easy, wasn't it?" she said quietly.

I didn't move.

She looked down at her lap. "But then again, no one ever said I could act, did they? Lots of critics say just the opposite."

I blinked several times and my shoulders tensed. "I—" I stammered, "I don't understand."

"Close the door, Piper."

I did and then pulled up a stool, feeling deceived and confused. "I ought to go get my parents."

"Oh, don't do that, Piper." Her eyes widened. "Please."

As the fact began to sink in that a movie star was staring at me in the flesh, one whose deception had cost me my first assignment (and possibly my job), I heard myself say, "I really needed those pictures."

She looked down. "Those pictures would have been pointless. There are enough glamor pictures of me to last a lifetime."

"They wouldn't have been pointless to me!"

"You want an exclusive, Piper?"

I nodded.

"Alright, then you go take a picture of Ferguson inspecting a bomb shelter, or Mrs. Butterfield canning vegetables, or your father taking care of the refugees from London, or your mother and aunt taking care of the Jewish children from Europe. Now those are some pictures worth taking!"

"Nobody prints pictures of Mrs. Butterfield or Ferguson."

"Well they should." She glared at me.

I met her gaze right on. "I want to know why you lied."

"First," she paused, "you tell me how you figured out who I was."

"It didn't take a rocket scientist. Lois is supposed to be in Kingsbarns. Then it's reported she's sick. Then there are rumors that she is flat-out missing. I over-hear you talking to someone on the phone, and it's definitely *not* about a missing trunk."

"You'll make a great reporter yet." She grew

nervous. "Piper, please, none of this can make it back to your editor."

"Why did you lie to us, Golda, or Lois, or whoever you are?"

"I never lied. Actually, it's the first time in a long time I was telling the truth about myself." She paused briefly before confessing, "Well, I did lie about the trunks. I was calling my assistant to get the police off my tail. I have no desire to be found."

"Golda Meyerson?"

"My name. My passport." She laughed without smiling. "The studio changed it because it was too Jewish."

"Lavigne sounds pretty Jewish."

"It means 'vineyard' or something in French. The Jewish spelling is different. L-E-V-I-N-E."

I rolled my eyes. "And all that rot about being twenty-six years old and growing up in France?"

"Made up. They thought I needed a more exotic background. Something European and sophisticated. They stuck fake teeth on a clip and took my glasses off, and now that I'm getting older they tape my scalp back to hide the wrinkles." She inhaled and demon-strated. "I'm not allowed to grow up, see? And Lois is a vegetarian only because she can't say she's kosher, now, can she? She might lose her job if the public knew she'd been lying to them for ten years."

She released the skin around her face and tilted her head to the side. "I did work in service, Piper. I stopped school when I was sixteen and worked as a maid in a very fine house in Philadelphia. One day, when I was twenty-one, a studio executive from Hollywood came to dine. I had always liked movies, ever since I was very little. My mother loved Shakespeare and taught me what she could. She wanted me to be on the stage and trained me to speak properly. But I preferred movies. I knew films were powerful, wonderful tools, evoking the deepest emotions of the human soul. I wanted to be a part of something so glorious, so provoking, so important." She looked back in the mirror. "The studio executive liked my looks. . . he said that I might have what it takes. The rest is history, as they say."

I sat, rooted on the stool.

"So you see? I am Golda, and I am Lois. But not anymore. From now on, I'm only Golda."

"But why this charade? Why run away?"

"I hate those movies I've played in. They won't let me make the movies I want, and I never want to play in another musical again."

"I like your films," I protested. "I think they make a

lot of people happy, and people need happiness right now."

"You are very sweet to say so. But I joined this business to do more than make people happy."

"And why can't you make the movies you want? You are a big star! You could be in anything you want, couldn't you?"

"Do you know what the term 'blackballed' means?"

I shook my head no.

"In general, it refers to the process of being excluded or denied the right to work. When I said a job didn't work out, I was telling the truth."

"Go on," I said. The newspaper woman in me felt a story. My fingers itched for the camera.

"Off the record?" she asked again.

Reluctantly, I nodded.

"A man brought me a script," she said, leaning forward. "It was brilliant. It was about Berlin and the rise of the Nazis and the awful oppression of the Jewish people. And it all centered on a beautiful love story between a German Christian girl and a Jewish lawyer. It was a wonderful film. A natural hit. Oh, Piper, I couldn't find one producer or studio willing to make it! I pushed hard. I went to every producer I knew. And I know a lot. Not one was willing to move forward."

She inhaled, "Then the head of my studio called me in for a little chat."

"A little chat?" The way she said made it sound ominous.

Drumming her fingers frustratedly, she continued, "He made it abundantly clear that the studio won't make any movies that might encourage the American people to go to war in Europe. Even if they are true! Instead, they are making movies like *Gone With the Wind*, even while the threat of the Nazis looms right on our doorstep!"

"American studios won't make movies about the Nazis?"

She nodded. "Oh, they made three or four. There was *Confessions of a Nazi Spy*, which was fine but cheap, and the story stunk. And *The Great Dictator* which was brave but missed the mark. Just between us, I'm all for comedy when it comes to satire, and Chaplin is a genius, but he just didn't go far enough!"

"Well, that is something," I offered, thinking back to the conversation I'd just had with my parents."

Golda shook her head. "It's not enough! As soon as the war began, any effort to show what's happening in Europe or was seen as too 'pro-British' was shut down with a resounding boom." As if on cue, a roll of thunder sounded outside the window.

"It rains here a lot." She glanced at the curtained window.

"Welcome to Scotland." I sighed.

"Anyway," she continued, "I found out that the studio fired all non-Aryan employees in their German offices."[1] A tear fell down her cheek. "I told the head of my studio that he had to hire them back, or I would go to the papers."

I waited.

"And he told me that if I went to the papers, he would make sure I never got a job in Hollywood again. He said I had no real proof those people were fired because they were Jewish, and no one would believe me anyways. What's worse, he threatened to tell everyone all about who I really am—how old I am and my real name and so forth—if I went ahead and broke the story." She looked down. "If everyone found out how I've been lying in that way, it would ruin my career."

She held her breath a second before exhaling slowly. "And then I told him I would quit."

My eyes widened. "And he told you?"

"If I quit, he'd sue me for breach of contract." A tear trickled down her face. "This last movie, *All That is Gold Does Not Glitter*, was the last straw. I'm done Piper. I don't want to be Lois anymore. Lois is accosted by crowds of people who only want her autograph. They don't want to hear what she has to say, not really. They just want to see her sing and dance, which is pointless. And Lois belongs to a studio who refuses to do what's right. They, the ones with the loudest voices in the world, the movie studios, won't. . . won't. . ." Tears began to fall harder. "I don't care if I break my contract. I'm not going back to work with people who won't stand up for what's right. People who are afraid to tell the truth and do the right thing. People who let the Nazis call the shots!"

"Wow." This stunned me.

"Quite a story, huh?"

I nodded, thinking what a shame it was I'd agreed for the whole thing to be off record and desperately wishing I was more than a mere photographer.

"Believe me, the minute America joins the war, Hollywood will change her tune. But not before, not when it matters most. Those producers and studio heads will always choose what sells. If the Nazis intimidate them and say jump, they ask how high. And they'll hang all us out to dry. At least for now. Like I said, if America joins the war, things will change. Money follows public opinion. And public opinion is made with money. It's a humiliating, vicious cycle." Golda frowned deeply. "There's even talk of a Senate subcommittee who is preparing to launch an investigation."

"Into what?"

"Into whether the studios are creating pro-interventionist films—you know, films to inspire America to help end Nazi terror. It's a prospect the Senate finds very, very concerning because so many of them don't want a war. They don't need to worry though," she groaned. "Most Americans don't want to risk their lives for others either. Most *people* don't want to risk their lives for others. But there is no such thing as 'peace at all costs.' Someone always loses something when that phrase gets tossed around. Things like free speech and freedom of expression."

She looked down, and it was impossible for me to read her.

"Couldn't you find those in Hollywood willing to make a difference in their films?"

"Oh, they're there. But they can't get funding. And now, with this Senate committee, the films might never get to be shown—" (I knew *this* was the kind of censorship that worried my mother.) "—And let's just imagine I could get the funding and the people, my boss said he would make sure I never worked in Hollywood again."

"Do you think he can really do that?"

"That mob boss?" She laughed and then squared her shoulders. "It's pointless. Besides, I'm exhausted by the crowds. Exhausted from the superficiality of it all. I want to be a real woman again. Gap teeth, smile lines, and all."

"So you've given up."

She didn't answer. "I don't have another choice, do I?"

"And you are just going to stay with us as Golda Meyerson and let Lois Lavigne fade away?"

"At least Golda Meyerson is useful, not merely decorative."

Neither of us spoke for a moment as the rain pelted the window. Her face, aged more by stress than actual age, was the face of a woman trapped between a rock and a hard place. Her conscience wouldn't let her continue a career of meaningless silence, but the "forces that be" wouldn't let her speak the words she wanted to. In the end, her decision was to leave that woman behind all together and once again become Golda.

"Oh my, Golda." I sighed sadly. "You are in a jam, aren't you?"

"No," she shook her head, "I'm not in a jam. All those kids in Germany are in a jam. Not me. If anything, I'm better than I've been in years. I feel like

I have a chance for the first time since I can remember.

"They'll find you, you know, eventually. Fans have a way of doing that."

She shook her head. "No, they won't. My personal assistant is taking care of everything."

"Don't you think she'll tell?"

"I never told her where I am! For all she knows, I went back to London."

"I see." A moment passed before I asked, "Why don't you want the family to know?"

"They treat me like me. . ." She reached out and grasped my hand. "And you *mustn't* tell Ferguson. Promise?"

I looked into her deep brown eyes. They were so sad. And so lonely. And, despite the frantic energy she'd shown through the day, dog tired.

7

The Next Day

Once again, I awoke to the pipes. My pocket Bible was still open to 1 Peter 4:10-11. *"Each of you should use whatever gift you have received to serve others, as faithful stewards of God's grace in its various forms."*

I peeked out the window at the school boys jumping up and down. There was Horatio, right there with them. Ferguson was likely in bed and would be getting up just now too. On nights he was on duty, he'd come home at 5:00am, just as the sun began to rise. Then he'd doze off for two hours and be up and at em' again. The house couldn't run without him. And he pretended he could run without sleep.

There was a dull thudding pain in my head, probably because I went to bed much too late.

Down in the kitchen, I accepted my oatmeal from Mrs. Butterfield along with my daily scolding. My mother, Edie, and Anna (and Fanny the monkey) were all in their places. And then came Golda. *She* didn't look tired at all.

"Good morning, Miss Piper." She gave me a knowing look. We both had a secret. I still wasn't sure she should keep it. Then again, it wasn't my secret to share, was it?

"Golda," Edie cried out, "put that basket of laundry on the floor and sit down and have a cup of coffee with me and Rose."

"And me," I said.

"And me!" Anna repeated.

"It goes without saying," Edie motioned towards a chair as Mrs. Butterfield shot my aunt a disapproving, look clearly communicating she didn't think it was proper for the help to have breakfast with the mistress. Of course, Mrs. Butterfield had extra generosity towards my aunt, given she was an American and used to doing her own housework. She (in Mrs. Butterfield's opinion) just didn't understand the way things were done.

Edie held her stomach and leaned forward. "Golda Meyerson. You are not a maid."

"What?" Golda blanched and looked at me. I tried to wordlessly convey that I hadn't said a word.

"You are an artist," she went on. "A great one! Possibly one of the greatest."

"I. . . I, uh. . ." Golda stammered. "Thank you."

"Now, you are still undeveloped. Your ideas are forming."

"Where's dad?" I cut in, trying to change the subject.

My mother answered, "Edie insisted he go straight to the village and examine Miss Lois Lavigne."

At this point, Golda realized her secret was still safe. Everyone at the table, except for me, accepted that Golda was Golda, despite her uncanny resemblance to Lois. It struck me how influential the power of suggestion really was. She exhaled a sigh of relief.

"Ma'am," Golda said, "I just enjoy going to the movies."

"Enjoyment is the first sign of great talent, my dear!" She shook her head. "Take it from me. I'm a writer! I know the throes of passion and joy that come with doing what you love—the ecstasy, the despair! Ask Rose! She's a writer too."

My mother blinked. "I was just a journalism student, Edie. And the writing I did in school is nothing like the writing you do. It was much less. . . dramatic."

"Oh, Rose! Don't disparage yourself like that. You could write dramatic prose with the best of them. If you'd just push yourself!"

"Edie, please," my mother said. "Don't excite yourself."

Edie waved my mother's warning off with the flick of a hand. "As I was saying, you'll need to embrace risk!"

"Risk?" Golda repeated.

"Your job, for one thing. You can't spend all day doing the laundry. You must carve out time to hone your skill! And then you have to risk that no one will like what you write, but you write it anyway because you must and if you don't, you'll die! And let's not even talk about relationships! Characters running amuck in your head can be very distracting when someone is talking to you at the supper table."

"Edie," my mother groaned, "you'll make her run away from any sort of creative work with a speech like that."

"I just want her to know what she must be willing to face!"

"Oh, believe me, I'm quite terrified. Rest assured I

could happily stay in service forever. Or get married and have a family. I'm thirty-six years old!"

"Oh, tish tosh." Edie let out a laugh. "I wasn't married till I was forty. You've years and years to go before that. Not to say if you meet someone wonderful you shouldn't marry him, but. . . in the meantime, why not run full throttle after what God made you to do?"

"I'm a maid," Golda answered flatly.

"But you're not meant to be! Some people are like me. I am blessed with the ability to perfect my craft, have a family, and clean. . . when I'm not pregnant, that is. But not everyone is so gifted. Mrs. Butterfield, for instance." Edie was dead serious. I closed my eyes, a bit embarrassed. "Lois, I love that you want to serve my family, but your gift lies another way, and you must choose your focus and run with it. Reach for the stars!" Edie froze and then put a hand on her side. "Ouch." Then she kept going. "My only critique, of course, I haven't seen your work yet, is that you might need more levity."

"Levity?"

"Lightness, laughter, comedy! People need comedy, especially if you want them to listen to you! You mustn't take yourself too seriously!"

"Well, Edie," Golda said playfully, "I'll be honest. I am not a writer. It doesn't come naturally to me."

"Me either." I sighed.

"A painter then?" Edie suggested.

Golda shook her head as a tiny smile graced her lips. "Maybe an actress?"

Edie slammed her hand against the table. "Why didn't I think of that! After your brilliant performance last night as the ill-fated Scarlett O'Hara! You could apply to the London Academy of Arts! Or better yet, take up method acting. I hear it's much more modern." Once more, she gripped the table and shouted, "Ouch!"

"What's the matter?" Golda asked as we all leaned forward.

"Now don't put off what I said, Golda, just because I feel a slight pinch." She grimaced. "Indigestion probably. But you are going to need a benefactress, and I plan for her to be me!"

"Maybe you ought to go lie down." My mother's forehead creased with concern, and she stood to help Edie upstairs. "Golda," she commanded, "you take her other arm. I'm worried about managing the stairs alone."

"And if you should choose to be an actress, Golda, you must aim for the stage. You look too much like

Lois Lavigne to make it in pictures." My aunt's voice continued as they moved out of the kitchen, leaving Anna and me all alone.

"Well, Anna," I smiled at the little girl, "looks like it's just you and me."

"And me," Ferguson said, wearily entering the kitchen. He took a cup of coffee from Mrs. Butterfield and sat next to me in the seat Golda had just occupied.

"What did you find out?" he leaned in and whispered.

"Her name is Golda Meyerson, Ferguson. She was born in Philadelphia. She's thirty-six, and she did work in service for years."

"Really?"

I nodded.

He sipped his coffee, visibly relieved Golda was not a spy or a criminal on the run. "I'm glad to hear that. We need the help. Still," he shook his head, "at a time when every able-bodied woman is working in a factory, why would she choose to work for us?"

Quickly, I tried to think of how to protect Golda's secret without fibbing. "She said," I swallowed. "She said she was going to complain about a bad boss, and he threatened to blackball her if she told anyone what he had done. . . or something."

"Threatened to blackball her?" Ferguson's voice was edged with concern.

"He said he would make it hard for her to ever get work in her old town again." I could feel my brow creasing.

"It sounds like she needs a lawyer. The workplace can be very difficult to navigate if you don't know your rights! Poor Golda." A genuine sadness filled his eyes. He clearly cared.

"I think a lawyer is a great idea. But I also happen to know she could really use a friend."

He blushed slightly. "Yes, a friend…" He hesitated and then added, "Did you ask her? About the walk this afternoon?"

I froze. I had completely forgotten. I looked up just as Golda walked in. "You'll just have to ask her yourself."

"Ask me what?" She tilted her head to the side.

Ferguson awkwardly hesitated and coughed. "I was, well, I was going to ask if you're free this afternoon?" It was becoming more obvious by the minute how much he liked her, though he'd only known her less than thirty-six hours.

"Free to what?" she answered innocently.

"Oh, I was thinking I could show you around Kingsbarns, given you are new here."

"Oh my!" It was her turn to blush now. "Why, that would be wonderful. But, one village is like another. Why don't we take a walk in the hills?"

"I would find that most pleasant." He looked at the table, unable to look at her straight on.

"How's Edie?" I asked.

"She said the pain subsided and something about not being able to handle coffee the way she used to. Your mother is staying with her awhile." She turned to Ferguson, "And what, may I ask, sir, are you doing up? You were up all night!"

"If I'm not mistaken, it is 9:00 in the morning, Miss Meyerson. In my book, the day is nearly done."

"And in my book, two hours of sleep for the most important man in this house is ridiculous. You must take care of yourself, Ferguson."

Something about the way she said it was so sweet, so fetching, that Ferguson was left completely unresponsive, like he'd been shot dead center in the heart with Cupid's arrow.

"You are tired. Please," Golda implored quietly, "let me help you."

As he opened his mouth to answer, the sound of my mother's panicked voice took all of our attention.

"Nathan! Nathan!" she shouted, running into the kitchen.

"Whatever's the matter, Mrs. Gordon?" It was Mrs. Butterfield talking from her domain near the stove.

"Is your father back yet?" she asked me directly.

"No, he's still with Lois Lavigne, remember? Food poisoning?"

"Ferguson," her eyes were wide, "you must go fetch him immediately! And someone find Horatio! Edie's going to have her baby!"

Mrs. Butterfield dropped her spoon on the ground and exclaimed, "Saints preserve us," as Ferguson dashed out the door.

"What do we do now?" I asked, my heart pumping wildly.

"Boil some water!" Mrs. Butterfield shouted.

"Why?" I asked.

No one answered me.

"Yes, yes, boil the water!" Golda agreed. "And we'll need clean sheets, lots of them!" She followed my mother out of the kitchen, shouting over her shoulder, "Bring them up as soon as possible, Mrs. Butterfield, watch Anna! Come along, Piper, I might have need of you!" (I'll admit I thought it strange she didn't ask Mrs. Butterfield to help her, but it was a dramatic moment. No one was thinking clearly!)

When we arrived at my aunt's door, she was in bed groaning. "Where's Horatio! Where's Nathan!" she cried. "My own brother—a doctor and a resident of my house, and he's not even present at the birth of my first child!"

"Dr. Gordon is on his way, ma'am." Golda threw the thick window shades apart and light streamed in, filling the beautiful room with the morning sun. The thick oriental carpets, the dark wood floors, and heavy oil paintings made for an opulent room, filled with carefully curated pieces from Horatio's many travels.

"Where's Horatio!" she cried again.

My mother shouted, "I'll go find him!" and rushed out.

I looked at Golda and explained, "My mother is a very brave woman, but she doesn't do well with the sight of blood."

"She married a doctor!" Golda cried.

I shrugged.

Again, Edie shouted out.

"Not to worry." Golda helped her stand. "Walking can help. And then we'll massage your back. That can help too." She put her hand on my aunt's shoulder, "And breath slowly. Yes, like that. Excellent."

"Are you a midwife too?" Edie asked, biting her lip.

"No."

"Have you ever helped deliver a baby?" I asked, also

surprised at Golda's confidence and coolness under pressure.

"I played a midwife in a movie." Golda stopped as Edie doubled over.

"You what?" Edie gasped.

"I played a midwife in a movie," Golda repeated. "To learn the role, I studied midwifery. Method acting, you know."

Edie's eyes widened. "You're not—" Before she could finish, another pain seized her.

"Oh my." Golda swallowed. "This baby's almost here! Piper, go find Mrs. Butterfield, your mother, anyone!"

I dashed out, wildly searching through the house, yelling for my mother. Mrs. Butterfield, sheets in one hand, a pot of boiling water in the other, rushed past me on the stairs. "Where's Anna?" I cried, still running.

"Don't you worry about her, Miss Piper. I dropped her off with the boys upstairs. Mr. Chatham" (one of the tutors) "was happy to watch her."

I heard the front door swing open, and Horatio and my mother dashed up the stairs. Neither so much as looked at me.

As another one of Edie's cries shook the house, I froze. Where was my father?

On cue, the Rolls appeared with Ferguson at the helm. As he gunned the car to the front door, my father jumped out. "How is she?" he shouted, his black leather doctor's bag in hand. "To think," he went up the stairs two at a time, "I never leave this place, and the first morning in nine months I go into town, for a woman who wasn't even there, mind you, my sister goes into labor!"

"What do you mean, wasn't there?" I called up.

He glanced at me. "Lois Lavigne is no longer in Kingsbarns. The desk clerk informed me that her assistant checked out for them both early this morning."

Ferguson huffed behind me. "Your poor aunt, she had her heart set on meeting Lois."

"Maybe she already has," I answered as we reached my aunt's room. Horatio was outside the door, nervously wringing his hands.

"Stay here, Piper," my father told me just as my mother opened the door and stepped out.

"How is she?" my father asked, pausing for a moment.

"She's fine." My mother was flushed and excited. "And so is her mother. You missed it, Nathan." She turned to Horatio. "You have a beautiful, healthy girl."

"And my Edith?"

"Right as rain." She beamed. "You're a father!"

She held the door open, and we followed my father inside. There was Edie in bed, looking hot, exhausted, and happy. Mrs. Butterfield was wiping her brow, and there was Golda, a little bundle wrapped in a clean sheet, walking towards Horatio.

"I want you to meet your daughter, sir. Little Agatha Macleay."

"You named her after me?" I felt a tear spring to my eye.

Horatio nodded. "We agreed on Agatha for a girl and Samuel for a boy."

"Agatha Golda Macleay," Edie corrected from the bed.

Golda blushed a little and caught Ferguson's eye. "Looks like you did a very good service here today, Miss Meyerson." Ferguson also blushed.

"Bring me my baby, Horatio!" Edie sat up a bit as Mrs. Butterfield fluffed her pillows. "And, Piper, go get your camera. I want to commemorate this moment! All of us together!"

"No, no, no," my father protested. "I want to do a full examination of you and the baby first."

"Oh, Nathan, I feel fine! I'm as strong as a horse. Everyone knows that."

"No arguments, Philipa Edith."

My father took the baby from Horatio and smiled. "How's my little niece?"

Horatio sat next to Edith and held her hand.

"I want to know how Lois Lavigne was? Was she ever so grateful for your expert attention?" my mother asked with a hint of sarcasm. Edie, Golda, and I looked at each other.

"She wasn't there," he said, keeping his eyes on little Agatha.

"What?" Horatio frowned.

"She wasn't there," my aunt breathed, "because she was somewhere else."

"Obviously." My father had his stethoscope out and was listening to the baby's heart.

"Well, where was she?" Standing up, Horatio looked over my father's back at his daughter. "Is she supposed to be all red and wrinkled like that?"

"Quite normal," my father assured him. "Baby's color looks good. Lungs are strong. Very good."

"Here," Edie said.

"Here what?" Horatio turned back to his wife.

"Lois Lavigne wasn't there because she was here."

"You saw her?" My father took the stethoscope off and paused.

"You saw her too." The new mother reached out and took the baby back.

"I thought she was sick?" Horatio frowned.

"She feels just fine." Golda spoke from beside Ferguson.

The whole family, Ferguson included, turned and stared at Golda/Lois.

Edie sniffed. "Everyone, may I present Miss Lois Lavigne, a woman who is a much better actress than the critics give her credit for. I told you I knew she was coming. I just didn't know she'd already come. I just can't believe I didn't catch the resemblance! And I'm an artist! I study faces!"

"But I thought—?" Ferguson shot me a confused look. "You told me. . .?"

"She is Golda Meyerson," I explained. "Lois Lavigne is a stage name."

A great big bellow of laughter came from Horatio's belly, causing the baby to let out a wallop of a cry.

"Alright," my father shooed us out, "We'll get all this sorted later. For now, I want my sister and niece to rest."

Without hesitating, we all shuffled into the hall as my father shut the door behind us.

8

A Rising Star

I watched out my window as Ferguson and Golda sat on a bench at the end of the lawn. It was May 10, 1940, just a few days after Agatha Golda Macleay was born. A glorious sunset cast a greyish-blue light with streaks of orange and pink on the couple. They had been talking for hours every chance they could in the few days that had passed since the baby's arrival. Theirs was a profound friendship. Both were so much more than they appeared on the outside.

Golda's story came out in bits and pieces. And as a family committed to protecting Golda's privacy, if she wanted to stay, so be it. Even though she was also Lois Lavigne, and had a mansion in Pasadena and four maidservants of her own (and two gardeners), she was more than happy to follow behind Ferguson, doing whatever he said she should, and helping Edie with the baby. And the truth was that we needed the help almost as much as she needed a refuge.

It was a perfect arrangement, except for the fact that my editor would never assign me a real job again. He had it in his head that I botched the whole thing up, and nothing I could say or do would convince Angus that I was not the one at fault. My first exclusive was also, apparently, my last. But I had promised Golda I'd keep her secret, and I would rather never take a picture again than betray her confidence—even though it hurt me a little.

The trigonometry homework on my desk vied for my attention, but I couldn't concentrate.

I saw Ferguson check his pocket watch and stand up, helping Golda up after him. The two of them walked side-by-side back to the house. *It must be time*, I thought to myself. *My homework could wait. . . again. We were going to the movies!*

Fifteen minutes later, everything was in place; the paintings were off the wall in the study, and the couches and armchairs were lined up in rows. Mrs. Butterfield came in, a large bowl of popcorn and a pitcher of lemonade in hand. With that, Ferguson adjusted the projector and shouted for us all to be quiet.

Edie was thrilled. "It's just like really going to the movies, Horatio! Even better because I can wear my dressing gown!" She paused before adding, "Too bad we don't have a newsreel. If we did, it would feel just like the real thing."

Checking his watch, my father said, "It's 7:00 p.m. The BBC's evening broadcast is on. Why don't we turn on the wireless and give it a listen? Would that suit you, Edie?" He popped up and switched the radio on and tuned in the station.

"Today, May 10, 1940, at dawn, Hitler and his Nazi troops invaded France, the Netherlands, and Belgium. One hour ago, Prime Minister Neville Chamberlain resigned as Prime Minister. King George requested that Winston Churchill replace Chamberlain and form the new government. Churchill accepted."

"Churchill Prime Minister, eh?" Horatio stroked his thick beard as the newscaster's voice droned on about how in the USA, Spencer Tracy's new film *Edison* was meeting great critical acclaim. "Well, there's not an appeasing bone in Churchill's body. Things are about to get interesting."

"Shall I start the film now?" Ferguson asked.

"Why not?" Edie gave him a thumbs up, adjusted

the sleeping baby on her lap, and then looked at Golda. "I know you don't agree, Miss Meyerson, but it's at times like this that movies like yours certainly have their place. I just want to watch something that makes me feel like there is something right with the world."

"Watching me spinning like a top makes you feel there is something right with the world?"

"Yes. Maybe it's because I just had a baby, and I'm overly emotional, but yes."

I leaned in and whispered, "I know you keep kosher, Golda. Is it alright to watch a movie tonight? Doesn't the Sabbath start in the evening?"

"I'm not *that* kosher," she laughed and stared ahead at the screen.

The click click click of the reel buzzed in the background as Mrs. Butterfield passed out the popcorn, and Ferguson turned down the lights.

For the next hour and forty-five minutes, we watched as Lois waltzed and twirled and belted her lungs out. Some moments were genuinely funny. And yes, it did make one think that some things were still right in a world gone wrong. As I looked around the room, I noticed my family's faces. They felt it too. My father smiled wider than he had in weeks. Horatio laughed so hard I thought he might burst a blood vessel. And my mother swayed back and forth with the music and hummed gently.

"You'll love the end," Golda said as the grand finale neared. "We did this Charleston number right out of the twenties. Very authentic and fast."

"Show us, won't you, Golda?" I asked.

"Well," she hesitated., "I don't know. I'm not warmed up."

The music started and the Golda on the screen decked out in a flapper costume began to tap her feet.

"Oh, you must," Edie said over the increasingly loud music. "I'd dance if I could, but I'm a little preoccupied. Come on!"

Golda chuckled, stood up, and moved in front of the screen, getting Anna, Willem, and Raffi to join her. "Like this," she said, kicking one foot out in front of the other.

The music and dancers on the film behind her picked up to a frenzied pace. All over the screen, coeds were shaking and throwing their hands in the air.

"Dance with me!" Golda shouted at me and my mother.

We got up and started kicking and hopping. I felt more like a confused praying mantis than a jitterbug. Golda kicked her way over to Ferguson and pulled him along, much to his embarrassment, until "The

End" flashed across the screen, and we all burst into applause.

Golda gracefully curtseyed and collapsed into a chair.

"What a wonderful film." My mother laughed heartily. "I really enjoyed it!"

Golda shrugged. "Lots of people did."

"I liked the story," I said. "How the girl left Paris and went back to her farm in Illinois or wherever it was."

"She went back to where she belonged and doing what she was made to do. Even though she was a fine designer, she was a better farmer. She had to give up what she wanted in order to do what she should." Edie sighed. "Though I got the definite feeling that the French cabaret singer was going to follow her, and things might turn out all right in that department. I mean, why else have the whole world sing like that at the end?"

"It's called an 'up-ending.' It makes the audience feel good, even if the ending is sad." Golda answered, pushing a loose strand of hair back.

"Regardless," Edie stood up and passed the baby to my mother, "sometimes you have to give up what you want in order to do what you should."

"Are you trying to send me a message, Mrs. Macleay?" Golda sat up straighter and hid a smile.

"Don't laugh behind those sly lips of yours, Lois Lavigne or Golda Meyerson or whatever your name is. You may want to be here, but you are meant to be up there." She pointed to the screen on the wall.

"The movies I want to be in don't exist in Hollywood."

"Then make them exist!" Edie sounded exasperated.

"What do you mean?"

"I mean," she groaned, "make the movies you want to make. Start your own production studio. Hire your own writers. You've probably got gobs of money. And I'm sure Horatio might back a project or two if he believes in it."

Horatio hemmed and hawed, "Well, I—"

"They threatened to blackball her, remember?" I threw in before he could finish. "The head of the studio will expose her and ruin her career!"

"Her career is *already* ruined if all she does is peel potatoes every day." Mrs. Butterfield shook her head.

"Ah!" Edie was bouncing up and down in her chair as a light bulb went off. "But an *exclusive* is different from an *expose*!"

We all looked at her blankly.

"Don't you see!" she exclaimed. "If Golda was to expose herself, it wouldn't be an expose. It would be an exclusive."

"You mean, I should tell the world I was born Golda Meyerson?"

"If it's written the right way, you would only gain sympathy and stronger loyalty from your fans, my dear. Especially right now with the Nazi threat, everyone would understand! Why, if anything, they'll just love you more."

My mother nodded in agreement. "By telling the truth, you take away the studio's power to use the truth against you!"

"It's a rather brilliant idea," Golda said slowly. "And it may save my career, but it won't let me make the movies I want to make, even still. Remember the Senate Committee?"

"How many films do you have left on your contract?" It was my father speaking this time.

"Three." She shrugged. "About a year's worth."

"Finish your contract out," he said emphatically. "And while you do, find the girls and boys not intimidated by the Nazis or the Senate Committee, the ones determined to stop the Nazis from hurting more people."

"And we'll petition and push and push and push

some more until the truth is told." Edie slammed his a fist on the back of the couch.

"You are saying I should start my own studio?"

"I guess," my father blinked, "we are."

"You think I could?" She shook slightly, "I mean, you really think I could start my own studio?"

"Miss Meyerson," Ferguson shut off the projector, "you are the hardest working, most passionate woman I've ever met. If you can't do it, I don't think anyone can."

"But I want to stay here!" she cried out, looking from Edie to Ferguson and then to me.

My mother spoke soothingly. "I think Edie is right Golda. You are called to Hollywood, not to Kingsbarns."

Ferguson nodded slowly. "We all have our place in the battle against the forces of evil, Miss Meyerson. Mine is to serve this family and the community of the village. Yours is, well, it's on celluloid." He looked down. "And if Hollywood won't have you, Britain has a healthy little film industry of its own. And we make movies that say things here, even if we don't have theaters to watch them in Kingsbarns. The British anti-Nazi films are churned out weekly."

"The joy you just gave us, Miss Meyerson," Horatio said solemnly, "was truly priceless. If you promise to produce a few of these lighter comedies alongside your brilliant dramas exposing social ills, well, I can promise to back one or two films, within reason."

"Really?" she gasped, truly shocked.

"You may not understand, but as a sailor in His Majesty's Royal Navy, I can honestly say that these sorts of morale-raising pictures can keep a soldier from dipping into fear or depression. It lifts the spirit. We humans need both sides of the coin—truth told with gravity and truth told with levity, and a good actress can do both."

"You really think so?"

He nodded. "I fought in the Battle of Jutland back in the First World War, so believe me when I say that films like *Lovely Lady* can keep hope alive. They remind people what they are fighting for."

"Faith, freedom, and the American way." My aunt put her hand over her heart and bowed her head, seeming to have forgotten momentarily that Horatio was *Scottish*.

"I was thinking more along the lines of *innocence*, my dear."

"And of course, Golda," my mother looked at her kindly, "if you want to stay, you are welcome. But if you really want to make a difference in the way you said, if you really want to help stop the Nazis, go use your gift. Or at least try. Whether it's received or not is up to God. Staying here is a cop-out. It's quitting, hiding behind a shield of disappointment and frustration. Don't squander the connections, talent, and inspiration you have by peeling our potatoes. Free-speech is something to protect and fight for these days. Fight to tell the truth. Fight for us, Golda."

"You really think Lois Lavigne should go back?" She frowned and rubbed her temples.

"No. Only go back as Golda Meyerson. From now on, you must be completely yourself, without fear of directors, producers, or critics!" Edie exclaimed.

Golda sat stone still, looking at her hands in her lap.

"Golda," my father spoke again, "if this war goes on, and if it is as bad in Germany as the rumors say, will you regret not using your talent to help awaken America to the truth?"

She lifted her eyes to meet my father's. "I'd regret it till the day I died."

"Then you know what you must do, don't you?"

Her head nodded up and down and then turned slowly to me. "I think I missed an appointment with this young photographer. And I'd like to reschedule."

"You mean," I inhaled sharply, "we're on the record now?"

"Tomorrow morning, when the light is good." She glanced at Edie. "I have another story I want to tell."

"I'd be happy to help," Edie bowed her head.

"I would be glad to help as well," my mother added.

A quiet filled the room, a quiet that was charged with the prospect of Golda taking Hollywood and the Senate on single-handedly. The tap-dancing, singing, comedian extraordinaire. One of the few people with courage on the silver screen. It was a silence that made my insides tremble, and it was broken unceremoniously by the sound of the baby who began to fuss. "I suppose it's her bedtime," my aunt said distractedly. "Mrs. Butterfield, you'll take her to bed, won't you?"

"Is Golda going to stay?" Willem whispered to his brother, who shrugged in answer as Fanny crawled from one shoulder to the other.

"It's getting late," my mother said. "It's bedtime. Especially yours, Anna." She took the little girl's hand and led her upstairs.

But the rest of us were not quite ready to go to bed. There was too much leftover energy in the room.

"You know," Ferguson said, his hand on the projector, "if no one is sleepy, there's no reason we can't watch the reel again. We won't have access to another night like this for the foreseeable future."

"Brilliant, Ferguson, as usual!" Edie leaned back in her chair. "A double feature!"

"Of the same movie?" my father asked, raising one eyebrow and following my mother out of the room. "You all enjoy. I'm going to bed."

But I wasn't tired. I was wide awake, and I spent the next hour and 45 minutes once again watching Golda twirl around and sing, and marveling at how the last few days had unfurled.

9

Lavigne: "How She Happened"

> By the time this article appears, Lois Lavigne will have started back to Hollywood to resume her picture-making. But this time, she will be going back *not as Lois*, she will be going back as *Golda*, a good girl from Philadelphia who once cleaned houses for the rich and famous. She is leaving the people of Scotland, changed forever, for she is not the elegant European woman her studio deemed necessary for publicity. Rather, she is a real American girl. She likes apple pie and hamburgers and doesn't speak a lick of French! Everyone knows

America produces some the loveliest girls in the world. Who else is so free and fearless and self-reliant!?

'I decided it was about time I let the world know who I am, and the timing felt right,' Golda told us in this exclusive interview.

'At a time when family members abroad are being killed or fired for having a last name like Meyerson, I decided to wear my name with pride for all the world to see.'

And to that, we say, bravo, Miss Meyerson, for your bravery and courage!"

After this came a spread of photographs (taken by yours truly) with the following captions underneath them:

> In this photograph, you see Golda Meyerson and Mrs. Butterfield, a cook who feeds 40 young schoolboys who have been moved to the countryside to escape Nazi bombs falling on London.

Here is Miss Meyerson with her dear friend Edith Macleay and the German-Jewish refugees Mrs. Macleay rescued last summer on the Kindertransport. They have not heard from their parents in months.

And here is Miss Meyerson with Mr. Ferguson on an inspection of the Kingsbarns County's bomb shelters. Every man, woman, and child must do their part to stop the Nazi threat!

Here is Miss Meyerson looking very elegant while she teaches a drama lesson to the schoolboys.

In each of these pictures, Golda smiled with the gap in her teeth showing, the wrinkles about her eyes crinkling for the world to see. We all agreed she looked much lovelier with them than without. She looked like a real woman, someone who had something to say. The story ended with:

66 **In her own words, Miss Meyerson said, 'I think it is very important to show**

how I spent my vacation in Scotland. We Americans must be aware of what is happening and what could happen to us.' When asked if she was happy to be going back to America, she said, 'I know my duty, and it is to my fans. I will do everything in my power to tell them the best stories I can.' And this is the remarkable story of how Golda Meyerson came about. And mark these words, she is a force to be reckoned with."

The article and the photographs were already en route to Angus. I was back in business. My career (and Golda's) was saved. We had gone back and forth on whether we should discuss in the article what Golda said about the studio's firing of the Jewish employees in the German office, but came to the conclusion that they would deny it. We needed proof, and we couldn't go to Germany and get it, now could we? No. The best thing to do was to share what we could, the sort of story no one could argue with. And there was plenty of that story right in Kingsbarns.

We'd spent a full day doing the photoshoot all over the estate. Golda wanted to showcase the people she believed were worth showcasing, namely, everyone but herself. In this way, she could use her fame to expose what was happening in Europe without exposing herself to the studio's wrath.

"What could they be angry at me for now? Taking a picture with some refugees? Why," she laughed, "the studio loves publicity. I was only doing my part." She shrugged. I'm going back so they can't sue me for breach of contract. I spilled the beans on Golda so they can't use 'her' against me. And if they fire me for putting Jewish refugees and London schoolboys on the cover of the papers, so be it. I'll just get started with building my own studio. It will all work out in the end! And we'll face the Senate Committee if and when we have to. I'm not afraid to speak the truth."

"I certainly hope so, Golda." I pulled her in for a hug.

"Your mother and aunt did a very fine job with that article." She smiled sadly. "I won't lie though, a part of me is very sad to be going back. I feel very alone in this fight."

"We're behind you, Golda." Ferguson spoke reassuringly.

The three of us, Ferguson, me, and her, were standing on the train platform.

The whistle blew. She was traveling directly to London to catch her flight to New York. From there, she'd fly home to Los Angeles.

"You are a brave and dedicated woman, Golda." Ferguson reached out and took her hand.

"I'm only doing what I must do, like you."

"We all do what we must." Ferguson didn't let go of her hand.

"Write to me?" she asked. "And maybe, when this madness ends, I'll come back and visit?"

"Or perhaps," Ferguson looked down at her face, "I'll come visit you in California."

"I'd like that very much. You can whip my staff into shape!"

"I'm pretty sure you can manage that just fine on your own." He glanced up as the train's door swung open, and the conductor yelled, "All aboard!"

"I would like a picture," Golda said fervently. "Quickly! You have your camera, don't you?"

I nodded. I rarely left the house without it.

Ferguson stood by her side, shoulder's touching,

saying as I snapped the shot, "I'll send it to you once it's developed."

I slipped the camera strap back over my shoulder.

"Just for us," she said. "That one is off the record!"

"Family is always off the record." I grinned.

Once again, the whistle blew. But Golda and Ferguson didn't move.

When it blew the third time, Ferguson helped her up the steps, and we watched as she made her way through the train and sat at an open window.

"Go with God, Miss Meyerson. And may God bless you in all your endeavors," Ferguson said loudly.

"Oh!" she cried out. And then, suddenly, she popped up and ran back down the car and down the steps. Racing up to Ferguson, she wrapped her arms around his neck and kissed his cheek, whispering, "Goodbye!" Then she got just as quickly back onto the train as its wheels began to turn.

Her face appeared in the window once more and tears streamed down her face. "Goodbye!" she called again. And she stayed there, her hand raised in farewell until the train had chugged out of site.

We waited a moment more and returned to the car. Suddenly, I felt rather tired. Ferguson looked like someone had knocked the wind out of him.

"Home, Piper?" he asked after he gathered himself.

"Home."

He started the engine and pulled out of the station. Neither of us spoke. The hills and sheep and farmhouses whizzed by.

"I'm going to miss her," Ferguson said finally, speaking to himself as though this was a shocking revelation. "She is the first person I've ever known who I will truly miss. Goodness knows, if this war was over, I'd. . ." He didn't finish.

"She would too, Ferguson."

"You really think so?"

"I know so."

A little smile escaped his lips. "Long-distance relationships in wartime. Whatever shall we do?"

"Don't look at me. Peter and I aren't even allowed to get married for another year-and-a-half or so."

"Thank goodness for that." He laughed, and we drove through the fields and past farms and up and over hills. We opened the windows, and the breeze blew through the car. Both of us were lost in our thoughts. Just as the estate came into view, I shifted in my seat and wondered out loud, "What we'll do without her? She really was a big help."

"Keep serving right here, Piper. We'll both... keep

serving. And you'll finally have a chance to finish that trigonometry homework!"

Looking at him, I laughed out loud. And then Ferguson laughed too as we both stared into the future, wondering what adventures lay ahead.

NOTES

HISTORICAL NOTE

1. McKee, Robert. *Story*. USA: Harper Collins, 1998.

1. CHAPTER 1

1. "The Impact of WWII on Women's Work," *Striking Women.org*, Accessed July 8, 2020, https://www.striking-women.org/module/women-and-work/world-war-ii-1939-1945

CHAPTER 2

1. A term used to describe the Nazi's intense method of offensive warfare in the form of merciless airstrikes over Great Britain.

CHAPTER 4

1. The Jazz Singer, released in 1927, was the first full-length "talking picture," forever changing the film industry.
2. "Gone with the Wind Script," *Scripts.com*, accessed July 8, 2020, https://www.scripts.com/script/gone_with_the_wind_62.
3. Golda's speech is inspired from Robert McKee's chapter "The Story Problem" in *Story: Substance, Structure, Style, and the Principles of Screenwriting*, Harper Collins, 1998, pg. 11-32.

4. Edie's speech is inspired from Robert McKee's chapter "The Story Problem" in *Story: Substance, Structure, Style, and the Principles of Screenwriting*, Harper Collins, 1998.

5. Edie's speech is inspired from Robert McKee's chapter "The Story Problem" in *Story: Substance, Structure, Style, and the Principles of Screenwriting*, Harper Collins, 1998.

6. Peter Feurerherd, "The Dangers of Gone with the Wind's Romantic Vision of the Old South," *JStore Daily*, Accessed July 8, 2020. https://daily.jstor.org/the-dangers-of-gone-with-the-winds-romantic-vision-of-the-old-south/

CHAPTER 5

1. Jim Crow laws were state constitutional provisions that segregated public schools, places, transportation, workplaces, restrooms, restaurants, and drinking fountains between white and Black Americans. Jim Crow laws were enforced until 1965.

CHAPTER 6

1. "Wartime Hollywood," *Digital History*, Accessed June 8, 2020, http://www.digitalhistory.uh.edu/teachers/modules/ww2/wartimehollywood.html.

BIBLIOGRAPHY

Feurerherd, Peter. "The Dangers of Gone with the Wind's Romantic Vision of the Old South." *JStore Daily*. Accessed July 8, 2020. https://daily.jstor.org/the-dangers-of-gone-with-the-winds-romantic-vision-of-the-old-south/

"Gone with the Wind Script." *Scripts.com*. Accessed July 8, 2020. https://www.scripts.com/script/gone_with_the_wind_62

"Hollywood and Hitler: Did the Studio Bosses Bow to Nazi Wishes?" *The Guardian*. Accessed July 8, 2020. https://www.theguardian.com/film/2013/jun/29/historian-says-hollywood-collaborated-with-nazis

"The Impact of WWII on Women's Work." *Striking Women.org.* Accessed July 8, 2020. https://www.striking-women.org/module/women-and-work/world-war-ii-1939-1945

McKee, Robert. *Story.* USA: Harper Collins, 1998.

Moser, John. "**Gigantic Engines of Propaganda**": **The 1941 Senate Investigation of Hollywood.** *The Historian.* **Vol. 63, No. 4 (SUMMER 2001), pp. 731-751. Accessed July 8, 2020.** https://www.jstor.org/stable/24450496?seq=1

"Wartime Hollywood." *Digital History.* Accessed June 8, 2020. http://www.digitalhistory.uh.edu/teachers/modules/ww2/wartimehollywood.html

ABOUT THE AUTHOR

Jessica Glasner is an author and screenwriter. Young and old alike agree that her lively characters, colorful settings, and laugh-out-loud vignettes display the goodness of God in the darkest moments of the past. Known for instilling hope, faith, and godly values through page-turning stories, inspiring tears and laughter, her books are those that are read over and over.

For more adventures with Piper and the gang, check out *The Seabirds Trilogy* on Amazon and Barnes and Noble.com.

facebook.com/jesskateglasner
instagram.com/jesskateglasner

Made in the USA
Middletown, DE
30 October 2020

23053435R00078